Starte pg 11.

Beat the Turtle Drum

CONSTANCE C. GREENE

Illustrated by Donna Diamond

A YEARLING BOOK

A Yearling Book

Published by
Dell Publishing Co., Inc.
1 Dag Hammarskjold Plaza
New York, New York 10017

Yearling ® TM 913705, Dell Publishing Co., Inc.

ISBN: 0-440-40875-X

Reprinted by arrangement with Viking Penguin Inc.

Printed in the United States of America

Sixth Dell printing—March 1985

CW

In memory of my mother and my father

Contents

O dance along the silver sand,
And beat the turtle drum,
That youth may last for ever
And sorrow never come.

IAN SERRAILLIER

May

My sister Joss is saving up to rent a horse. A man named Mr. Essig over in West Norwalk rents them by the week for thirty dollars. Joss has seventeen saved. Her birthday is next month. She tells everyone she doesn't want any presents. Just money.

Joss is going to fix up the garage for the horse to live in. Mr. Essig, though not a person to warm the cockles of my or anyone else's heart, will throw in some hay for free. He'll also van the horse to and from our house.

Mr. Essig looks like a member of the Mafia, only he's poor. He also looks like a gypsy. He has thick black hair all over him. That is, the parts you can see. He also has a gold tooth and a big scar running from his eyebrow to his mouth. He wears tall black boots and a scarf around his head. My mother says he's playing to the balcony in that outfit.

Joss thinks Mr. Essig is the neatest man. She rides her bike over to his house every Saturday to check out the horses. He has five, in various stages of decay. They are the most beat-up-looking animals I've ever seen. When you're downwind of Mr. Essig's house, you can smell the horses mixed in with quite a lot of other smells. Mr. Essig's front yard is full of cars that don't run. He's got an old convertible with no wheels and a Volkswagen bus with no windshield. He's going to fix up the cars and sell them, he says.

Mrs. Essig is blowsy. I was delighted the first time she came to the door when Joss and I rang to ask if we could look at the horses. Mrs. Essig talks with a cigarette hanging from her mouth. She has such big breasts she can't button her blouse across them. Her hair is blond at the ends and dark at the roots. She has a heart of gold, I think. I'd never seen a truly blowsy person before I met Mrs. Essig.

Joss can wind people, especially my mother and father, around her finger. She has been working on renting a horse for more than three years. Naturally, she would rather buy one, but she's about given up on that.

My father agreed to the rental bit finally when Joss wore him down. He says where we live isn't zoned for horses, but for a week no one can possibly object.

Joss will be eleven next month. I'm almost thirteen. Oddly enough, we're very good friends. Not too many people I know can say that. It's a rare thing to be friends with your sister, especially when she's your parents' favorite.

My father and mother are totally unaware that Joss is their favorite. They'd probably get really mad if anyone suggested it. They treat us equally well. Or unwell, as the case may be. When my mother's prize Spode teapot was broken while Mrs. Hadley was sitting with us, we both got yelled at. Actually, it was my fault. I was warming it with hot water before we made tea, as the English do. It slipped and fell into the kitchen sink. Mrs. Hadley had told me about this quaint custom. You might almost say it was her fault the teapot got broken.

I'm perceptive about human relationships, which is a good thing. I plan on being a poet and a playwright when I'm twenty-one. Sooner, if I can manage it. Perception is essential for poets and playwrights. That's why I know if my parents had to make a choice between us, if one of us had to be sent through enemy lines to get help, I would be the one. Just as, if we were all in a boat and the boat capsized, and we had only one life jacket, they would put it on Joss. They wouldn't plan it that way. That's the way it would be.

Which is why it's even more unusual that Joss and I are friends.

I realize that what I've just said puts my mother and father in an unflattering light. I don't mean to do that. I love them. They are good people, reasonably compassionate and not too rigid in their ideas.

My mother worries about us too much. If we sneeze or cough even once, she puts us to bed and calls the doctor. If we're not home from school in fifteen minutes, she imagines us lying in the gutter, mowed down by a hit-and-run driver. Or dragged into a light blue car with Connecticut plates by a man with slick dark hair and peculiar eyes.

My father is too impatient. He flies off the handle much too easily, and he doesn't let me finish my explanations of things. I've noticed he gets mad when someone interrupts *him*, however.

Outside of these failings, they're all right. To expect people to be perfect just because they're adults and/or parents is unrealistic, I think.

Last Sunday Joss decided to build a proper barn for her horse.

"What horse wants to live in a garage?" she asked indignantly. Probably this was due to the fact that we'd seen a television program about ranching in Wyoming, where no self-respecting horse would've been caught dead sleeping in a garage.

"We could tear down that old shed in back of the Smiths'," Joss said. "It can't be that hard to build a barn. A small one, that is."

Joss called up everybody she knew. "If you help, you can have a ride," she promised. A girl in Joss's class said she wasn't allowed to do manual labor on the Sabbath.

"All right for you," Joss said darkly.

The Collins twins, Ellen Spicer, my friend Sam Brown, and Tootie Simms showed up. Tootie is eight. He lives two houses down from us. He's big for his age and not the brightest kid on the block. When Joss had a strep throat last year, he sent her a handmade get-well card that said: "To Joss. The Best Person I Know. I Love You. Tootie." Joss still keeps that card in her top drawer. She didn't show it to anyone. Only me.

Everyone arrived wearing their old clothes and an expectant air. The twins each carried a rusty hammer. Tootie had filched a bag of new nails from his father, and Sam had a set of blueprints he said might come in handy.

"They were originally for a bomb shelter my grandmother was going to build about twenty years ago," Sam explained. "Then she moved to a condominium in Florida instead."

Joss told me later that she thought the horse might freak out if it knew it was living in a bomb shelter, but she thanked Sam. "They're very handsome," she said.

We all trooped to the woods in back of Smiths' and tore down the old shack. It was on its last legs anyway and didn't require much effort. Tootie got a splinter in his hand as big as a toothpick. It was so big, in fact, it was easy to pull out. Tootie was very brave. He closed his eyes and hung on to me while Sam pulled.

"I didn't cry once," he kept saying for the rest of the day. I painted a big slash of Mercurochrome over the wound so he'd have something to show for it.

We lugged the boards back to our yard and started in. Tim Collins kept getting in everybody's way. He also kept hammering his fingers instead of the nails. "I'm leaving," he finally said in disgust.

"You always quit when the going gets rough," his brother George said. George had been born five minutes after Tim. He was more patient and tried harder.

After a while Ellen said she had to go wash her hair. She washes her hair frequently. Everyone started to snarl at everyone else. The sun was hot, and a bunch of wasps were giving us a hard time. I went up to the house for a bucket of water to drink. Sam tied a handkerchief around his forehead to keep the perspiration from getting in his eyes.

"I thought it was going to be easy," Tootie said. "You said it would be easy," he said accusingly to Joss.

"Listen, if you want something bad enough you have to work for it," she told him sternly. "How do you think our forefathers felt when they went into the wilderness and had to build log cabins and all that stuff? You think that was easy? Some forefather you'd make."

That shut Tootie up for a few minutes. Then he said, "I have to go to the bathroom."

Joss was hammering up a storm. "You can use ours," she said.

"My mother doesn't like me to use other people's bathrooms," Tootie said, backing off.

"Oh, yeah? You've used ours plenty of times," Joss said. Tootie didn't bother to answer. He broke into a run and disappeared from view.

"If that kid thinks he's going to ride my horse, he's nuts," Joss said crossly. By this time it was me and Joss and Sam and George Collins and a bunch of boards that looked like a falling-down shack, which is what they'd looked like in the first place. Except that now it was in our back yard instead of the Smiths'.

"Wait'll Dad gets a load of this," I said.

"Maybe he'll be late getting home and it'll be dark," Joss said hopefully.

Luck was on our side. The wind rose and lightning flashed. We went inside and watched while the rain started.

"Looks like a northeaster to me," Sam said. Whatever it was, when the sun came out, our barn was mostly lying on the ground in a sad little heap.

"We could try again tomorrow," George said.

After a small silence Joss said, "I don't think the horse will mind sleeping in our garage."

Sam took off his handkerchief and wiped his

forehead. "Yeah," he said, "we can make a sign that says 'barn' and tack it up over the door. He'll never know the difference."

Tootie came across the lawn. "I'm back," he said.

Joss put her hands on her hips and frowned. "You are what is known as a fair-weather friend, I'm sorry to say," she told him.

"Can I have a ride, Joss? Can I?" Tootie asked.

"I'll have to see," she said.

*J*oss and I share the long, narrow bedroom at the back of our house. Someday, if we ever move, we might each have our own room, but right now we share.

Sometimes I wish I had my own room. If only we had a garret, I would like a room there, like Elizabeth Barrett Browning or the Brontë sisters. I believe if one writes poetry in a garret, it frequently turns out better. However, until we buy a house that has one, I'll settle for bunking in with Joss.

Sometimes she shouts out loud in her sleep and wakes me. Other times she talks. Mostly about horses.

"Do you think it would be a good idea for me to buy a martingale for my horse?" she'll say. Or, "When I get my horse, I'll have to be very careful it doesn't eat snow. A horse can get colic from eating snow."

"Since you're getting it in June, I don't think there's too much chance there'll be snow on the ground," I told her. As for a martingale, I don't know what it is, so I reserve judgment.

Joss is my chief sounding board for trying out my poetry. If she has a fault, it's that she's too uncritical. She almost always says, when I'm finished, "That's lovely, Kate," in a sleepy voice. "I think you're a very good poet. I think when you're grown up, you'll be famous and people will read your poetry all over the world."

Only rarely does she say, "I don't get it. What's it mean?" That's usually when the poem is so deep I'm not sure I understand it myself. That's one of the primary dangers of a poet—being too profound. Some people like profound poems, but mostly, I think, they want to understand what they read.

I try to write middle-of-the-road poems, poems a child can understand but which are really very deep. It isn't always easy.

Last night Joss shouted out in her sleep so loud she woke me up. So I shook her until *she* woke up.

"Cut it out," I said. "You're making too much noise."

"I didn't make any noise," she mumbled, sitting up. She was asleep before her head hit the pillow.

This morning she didn't even remember. "You're crazy," she said when I asked her what she had dreamed about. "I don't dream. Only once in a while I dream I'm racing in the Kentucky Derby. Then when my horse comes in first and they hang that big horseshoe of flowers around his neck, he bucks me off and I go flying up into the stands. Then I usually wake up."

One of the really nice things about Joss is her eyes. They are very large and have enormous pupils. Around the edges of the pupils, they are blue or green or gray—whatever she wants them to be. They reflect her moods. I have heard that the eyes are the mirrors of the soul. Joss's soul stares out at the world every day of the week. Why shouldn't it? She has nothing to hide.

"Kate, do you ever think about dying?" Joss asked me. She was polishing the riding boots my mother had bought for her at the Salvation Army store. They are only a little too big and in very good condition. Joss stuffed tissue paper in the toes, and they fit her fine. She polishes them every day before school with special soap to restore the leather.

"No," I said.

That wasn't strictly true.

"Sometimes," I told her. "Why?"

"You know what they said in church last Sunday," Joss said. She bent over her polishing job, and her hair hid her face. "They said everyone was born and everyone dies."

I waited.

"That seems fairly obvious," I said when she didn't go on.

"Well, I've been thinking, and I don't believe that I'm going to die. Or you either, for that matter," she said.

"How about Mom and Dad?" I said.

"Oh, they're going to die years and years from now," she said. She was very serious. "When they are terribly old and don't care any more. After you and I are grown up, then Mom and Dad will die and it won't matter."

"How come we're not going to die?" I asked her. "What will happen to us? We'll go on living and stay young. All our friends will get old, and pretty soon we'll be younger than anyone on earth. We'll be playing hopscotch when we're ninety-five, for Pete's sake."

I tried to make her smile. She wouldn't.

"You remember when they said last Sunday that dying was just a beginning?" Joss's pupils were so huge they made her eyes look black. "A beginning of what, I'd like to know."

"Girls, you'll be late," my mother called.

"Joss, listen," I said, "it's one of those things that's practically impossible to explain. How do I know?"

Joss put her boots back in the closet tenderly, as if she were putting a baby to bed.

"I don't want to talk about it any more," she said.

"Who brought it up?" Just because Joss and I were sisters and friends didn't mean I couldn't get sore at her. "Just who the heck brought up the subject anyway?"

"Girls," my mother called again, "Tootie's here to walk to school with Joss. Get a move on."

Joss beat me down the stairs.

"Hey, Toot, what's up?" she said, getting her books from the hall table. She was reading *Misty of Chincoteague* for the eighteenth time. She brought it to school with her every day just in case she had some spare time to read. She could recite chapters from it the same way my father can recite "The Rime of the Ancient Mariner."

"I read the best book last night," Tootie told us. "It was so easy." He rolled his eyes. "You wouldn't believe how easy it was." Tootie was a slow reader. He came from a family of kids who devoured books the same way they ate potato chips—with great ease and appetite.

"Good for you," Joss said.

"It was so easy," Tootie went on, "that even my little brother couldn't read it."

I thought about what Tootie had said all the way to school on the bus, but I still couldn't figure it out.

*T*he only person who might possibly object when Joss rents her horse is Miss Pemberthy. She lives across the street from us in a big white house. I know it's none of my business, but that house is entirely too big for one person. I think Miss Pemberthy should take in foster children or something.

I mentioned this to my mother.

"Fat chance," she said.

Miss Pemberthy accused Tootie of pulling up her prize dahlia bulbs. Tootie, of all people. He wouldn't harm a dandelion, much less a prize dahlia. Miss Pemberthy called Tootie's mother and said if he didn't stay off her property, she wouldn't be responsible if he slipped off her stone wall and broke a bone or two. Tootie's mother said she got the distinct impression that Miss Pemberthy was thinking of greasing the stone wall to make it good and slippery for Tootie's benefit.

Miss Pemberthy was in the army in World War II. She was a sergeant, I think. Sergeants, I understand, are very domineering people. They wouldn't get to be sergeants if they weren't.

The sign in her driveway says: "NO TURNING IN THE DRIVEWAY."

Not "Please" or anything. Just "NO TURN-ING."

Miss Pemberthy likes to maintain the standard of excellence achieved in our neighborhood by constant vigilance. That's what she told my mother when our dog Hazel got into her garbage and spread it around a little. Hazel smelled the lamb bone way down at the bottom of the garbage pail. Hazel likes lamb better than anything. If Miss Pemberthy had just given Hazel the bone straight out, she could've avoided all that mess. My father made Joss and me go over and pick up all the junk from Miss Pemberthy's lawn.

All of which makes me think Miss Pemberthy might object about the horse.

"Miss Pemberthy isn't going to like it when you rent your horse," I told Joss.

"Tough beans," Joss said. She was adding up how much it would cost to buy a bottle of horse shampoo, containing lanolin and deodorizer, plus some veterinary liniment to aid in the relief of temporary muscle soreness due to overwork or exertion.

"It all adds up to a terrible lot," she said, sighing.

"Maybe you better forget the whole thing," I told her.

Joss made a fist which she shook at me. "You make me so angry," she said. "This is the dream of my life, to have my own horse. I would do it if I had to work like a slave for a whole year to get the money. It's my life's ambition."

"How do you know when a horse's muscles are sore?" I asked her, to change the subject. Usually Joss is calm, cool, and collected. Only once in a while does she go berserk—when I tease her about the horse and when she plays cards and does something stupid that causes her to lose. Then she clutches her forehead and staggers around the room, shrieking vengeance. When she does this, my father says she reminds him of Eleonora Duse, who was a famous Italian actress at the turn of the century. Before his time. He's heard plenty about her emoting, though, from his father.

"He limps, same as you and me," Joss said. She was explaining about the sore muscles. "You have to treat it with hot and cold compresses. Same as a human. They're a lot like humans, you know."

"I heard they were the dumbest animals going," I said. "They're so dumb they don't know enough to come in out of the rain."

Joss shrugged. "They like the rain," she said. "They like nature. If more people liked nature, this would be a better world."

I went to the telephone to call up Sam and ask him for the math assignment. Once Joss got started on nature and how people didn't appreciate it, she was a nonstop talker. I figure if conservation is still a big thing when Joss reaches maturity, she might major in it at college.

"Sam's not home now, Kate," his mother said. "He went to the library to do some research. I'll tell him you called."

"It's not really important," I said. Sam and I are a week apart in age. I'm older. When Sam gets feeling like a really big wheel, I remind him of the fact. It doesn't do much good. Sam is actually the smartest boy I know. Which is good because he's not much to look at. Sam is homely. He has about eight cowlicks that make his hair grow all funny, and he has to wear thick glasses. If you see Sam and his father and older brother together, it's comical, they look so much alike. I'm afraid there's not too much hope that Sam will get better-looking. On the other hand, with him I don't think it's going to make a whole lot of difference.

"Tell him I might call back," I said.

"Not between seven and eight, please," Sam's mother said firmly. Sam's father comes all over queer if his kids get phone calls during dinner, Sam says. Most times he's very even-tempered, but this is one thing that irritates him.

"O.K.," I said and hung up.

he next day was Saturday. After break-fast we rode our bikes over to Essig's. Mrs. Essig was on the front porch, shaking a rug over the railing. It was fascinating to watch. When she shook the rug, all the rest of her shook. Arms, chest, cheeks, and chin. I supposed her rear end was shaking too, but her jeans were so tight they held her in like a tourniquet.

"What's up, kids?" she called.

"We just want to look at the horses," Joss said. She had about decided on Prince. Prince whinnied when Joss called him. He also came when she called. Maybe the fact that she always brought him a treat—a carrot or apple or lump of sugar—had something to do with Prince's coming.

Mr. Essig came out of the old shed that served as a barn. "You kids make up your mind yet? Don't forget. One half when you decide, one half on delivery. I'm kinda short now. I could use the half if you made up your mind."

"I don't have the money yet," Joss said. She held out a gnarled carrot, and Prince came to the fence and ate it. "My birthday's not until next month. I'm getting the money then."

"Prince is everybody's favorite. Gentle as a lamb. Some horses kick, bite, like that. Not old

Prince." Mr. Essig smiled. That was quite a sight. He had about ten teeth in his head. They were broken and dark brown.

"I'll give you half as soon as I get it," Joss said.

Mr. Essig made a sweeping gesture with his right hand. "That's O.K., babe, I'll put a 'Reserved' sign on Prince so's nobody else'll get him. Don't you worry none. Bert Essig's as good as his word. Cross my heart and hope to die."

"Come on in and have a cuppa coffee," Mrs. Essig called to us. "I got a fresh pot on the stove, you want some."

Our mother has a thing about kids drinking coffee. She thinks it's bad for us, all that caffeine. We're not allowed to drink it at home. Actually, I don't even like coffee very much. But I could feel Joss tugging at my sweater.

"Let's," she whispered. "I want to. Please."

We went. Mrs. Essig swabbed down the kitchen table with a sponge. Their bathroom was right off the kitchen. I could hear the toilet flushing. A lady almost as fat as Mrs. Essig came out. She had on a lot of eye make-up and the most fantastically long eyelashes I'd ever seen. Her hair was black, as black as a raven's wing. Had I read that somewhere? If it was original, I might use it in my next poem.

"My girl friend Sheila. Sheila, this is Joss and

Kate. Pull up a chair and make yourselves homely.'' Mrs. Essig poured the coffee into mugs. ''Milk?'' she asked.

We said yes, please, and she put the carton on the table and shoved the sugar bowl toward us.

''That'll put hair on your chest,'' Mrs. Essig said. ''When I make a pot of coffee, I don't fool around.''

Sheila couldn't take her eyes off us. Especially Joss. We'd been taught that staring was rude. I discovered if the stared-at stares at the starer long and hard, the starer gives up. Not Sheila. She made me nervous.

Mrs. Essig asked me questions about where we lived, if we were the only two kids in our family. ''You date yet?'' she asked me.

''I go to parties,'' I said.

''I started dating when I was twelve,'' she said proudly. ''I could've passed for sixteen. I had a figure even then.'' She started to refill my cup.

''That was delicious,'' I said truthfully. ''Could I have just a half?''

''I know who you remind me of,'' Joss said suddenly, looking at Sheila. ''I've been thinking and thinking, and I know who it is.''

Sheila blinked. Those eyelashes were heavy. She could hardly get them back up off her cheeks.

''Who?'' she said.

''Elizabeth Taylor,'' Joss said. We'd seen

Who's Afraid of Virginia Woolf? last week on TV. "I bet people ask you for your autograph all the time."

It was like feeding a guard dog a piece of rare meat. The hostility drained out of Sheila in a rush. She smiled. Mrs. Essig laughed and laughed. Sheila frowned.

"You got yourself a friend for life, kid," Mrs. Essig said. "Another cup?"

"No, thanks, we've got to go," I said. Sheila ran her hands over her hairdo and smiled again. "Nice to meet you," she said to Joss. She didn't say anything to me.

We got on our bikes and rode away.

"Were you serious?" I asked Joss. "Did you really think she looked like Elizabeth Taylor? I thought she was a mess."

We stopped for a red light.

"I read somewhere that if you tell a person they're beautiful—well, they get beautiful," Joss said. "I wanted to see if it worked. She was better-looking when we left than when we got there."

The light changed. Pedaling up Comstock Hill took some work. When we reached the top, I thought about what Joss had said.

The next time I saw Sam, I'd tell him he reminded me of Paul Newman. If I knew Sam, he wouldn't buy it. If he even knew who Paul Newman was.

When I told Mrs. Essig I went to parties, I was exaggerating. In the past year I've been to one party. With boys, that is. Despite the fact that young people are supposed to grow up much faster than in my parents' day, know about sex and related subjects, and experiment with drugs and alcohol, I have led a very sheltered life. Along with almost all my friends. We're in the seventh grade, and only two kids I know have smoked pot. Nobody I know has an alcoholic mother or father. Five kids in my class have divorced parents, but once the initial shock was over, they handled it all right.

As for sexual experience, I can only speak for myself. I have had none. No boy has ever put the moves on me. And if one did, I'd belt him from here to the moon.

"Kate, you do know about how babies are born, don't you?" my mother said to me when I was about eight. She'd been slipping me hints for years. Now she was checking to see if everything had fallen into place in my mind. Actually the whole thing wasn't entirely clear. But I wasn't going to put both of us through that ordeal, so I said, "Sure, Mom," and she was so relieved she looked as if the dentist had just told her she didn't have any cavities.

Sometimes I feel fortunate that the vicissitudes of life have passed me by. On the other hand, I feel cheated too. If I'd been more exposed to the seamy side of things, I would undoubtedly write more realistic poems and plays. You take Eugene O'Neill or Tennessee Williams. I bet when they were my age they'd been around some, seen a few sights.

Once Sam and Joss and I were walking in the woods back of our house, near the parkway bridge. We found a whole bunch of dirty pictures. I suspect they were stashed there by Jim Schneider for future reference. Jim was always making suggestive remarks about girls' figures and stuff. His father subscribed to *Playboy* magazine, I understand. Anyway, I can still remember those pictures, even though Sam and I were about ten and Joss was eight. They were of people copulating. I'd never seen pictures like that, but somehow you just know, even at that tender age. We checked them all out carefully, to make sure we didn't miss anything.

Joss said, "Heck, I've seen plenty of animals doing *that*. If that's all there is to it, what's the big fuss about?"

We put the pictures back where we'd found them. First, we tore them in half neatly, though. That gave me a lot of satisfaction. Let Jim Schneider paste them back together if he wanted.

I think if the same thing happened to us today,

or at least to Sam and me, we might react differently. We might be more embarrassed. I don't know. It's just a thought.

I'm starting to keep a journal of my daily thoughts. I think it's good training and also may be useful when I start to really write. Just the other day I read a book review. The reviewer called it "crisp, natural, and persuasive." I only mention this because the author was seventeen.

Imagine having a book published at seventeen! Only four years older than I am.

I better get going.

"*Kate, will you run this package over to* Miss Pemberthy?" my mother said. "United Parcel left it here yesterday. She wasn't home, and he didn't want to take a chance on someone stealing it."

"Oh, Mom," I said. I didn't like going over there, for any reason at all.

"There's a good girl. Bread cast upon the waters," my mother said. Whenever she tried to con me into doing something I didn't want to, she said that.

The air smelled of apple blossoms and garden fertilizer. It wasn't a night to be mad at anyone. I took Miss Pemberthy's porch steps two at a time. Lucky I had on my sneakers. I planned to knock, drop the box, and run.

"Come in, come in," Miss Pemberthy said, flinging open the door. She must've been spying on me.

"The United Parcel left this at our house," I said. "My mother asked me to bring it over."

"Come in," she said again. As if I were mesmerized, I followed her into the dark hall.

"When one lives alone, one must be careful. It's so easy to resort to alcohol," Miss Pemberthy said. She had a pitcher half full and a cocktail glass on a table. "That's why I'm very strict with myself. One martini and one alone before my evening meal." She smiled at me. "What can I get you?"

I didn't want anything. All I wanted was to leave. Before I knew what had happened, she'd put a glass of ginger ale into my hand.

"Thank you," I said. "I really can't stay." If I didn't sit down, it would be easier to escape. I never could figure out why leaving a place you don't want to be in in the first place is so hard. "It's almost dinnertime."

Miss Pemberthy sat in her rocker and took a long sip of her martini.

"How old are you now, Kate?" Miss Pemberthy asked me. I hadn't known she knew my name.

"Thirteen," I said. "That is, I'll be thirteen in September."

"Thirteen," Miss Pemberthy said slowly. She took another sip and refilled her glass. That was some big martini.

"I was thirteen when my mother died. I remember it as if it were yesterday." Her eyes looked through me, past me, at something I couldn't see. "I made up my mind I would keep house for my father, make him forget, make him happy again.

"I tried very hard to make him happy. He got married less than a year after my mother died. He married a woman he'd known a short while. They shut me out. They forgot I was there. He always called my mother 'Dearest.' Now he called this woman, his new wife, he called her 'Darling.' "

"My father usually calls my mother 'Honey,' " I said. I sat down on the edge of a chair covered in a hairy brown fabric that scratched my legs. I didn't want to sit down, I just did. But then, I didn't want to feel sorry for Miss Pemberthy either, and I did. I wished she'd stop talking, stop telling me these things.

"When he teases her, he calls her 'the little woman.' She really hates to be called that. She gets mad." I laughed as if I'd said something terribly funny. "She jumps up and down and says, 'Stop that!' " Which wasn't true, but I said it anyway. I put my glass very carefully down on a table.

"He called her 'Darling' every time he turned around." Miss Pemberthy went on as if she hadn't heard me. "They kissed right in front of me. I felt I was in the way. It's a terrible thing, to feel in the way in your own house. My stepmother was kind to me. She wasn't wicked. He gave me money for books and clothes, but he didn't really know I was around." Miss Pemberthy emptied the pitcher into her glass. I got up and inched toward the door.

"I hear my mother calling," I said. "Goodbye," I said and ran.

The night was there, waiting for me. How glad I was to be out in it! I threw open my arms and ran, ran as fast as I could toward my own house. The lights were on, and in the dusk I could see my father coming up from the garage, his newspaper tucked under his arm.

I hurled myself at him.

"What's up?" he asked in surprise.

"Nothing, Dad," I said. I hugged him until he grunted.

"To what do I owe this display of affection?" he asked.

"I don't know," I said. "I just felt like it."

"*Joss*," I said, "*remember Jean-Pierre?*" Last night she'd had another of her bad dreams. I wanted to see if she'd remember the next morning. Sometimes she didn't. When she woke, her brain was washed clean of any memory.

"Sort of," Joss said. "I loved him a lot."

When Joss was small, around four or five, she'd had an imaginary friend named Jean-Pierre. Nobody knew where she got the name. We don't have any French ancestors. Jean-Pierre came everywhere with us—to the tree fort we built in the old apple tree in our back yard, to the bathroom where Joss had a terrible time making him brush his teeth, and even out to restaurants.

My father took us out for spaghetti Sunday nights to the Arrow Restaurant in Westport. You could eat at the Arrow until you burst and it hardly cost anything. The Arrow was my father's favorite restaurant. Not only was it cheap but you didn't have to dress up.

The first time we went, Joss told the waiter that Jean-Pierre needed a high chair. "He's not as big as me," she said.

The waiters at the Arrow are family men with experience. Nothing fazes them. This one brought a high chair and stood with his hands on his hips while Joss fitted Jean-Pierre inside. Then he handed Joss a big paper napkin.

"Better tuck this in good," he told her. "At that age they're awfully messy."

Joss said, "You are a very, very nice man."

People were looking at us and smiling.

"Don't slurp, Jean-Pierre," Joss said sternly.

One night we talked our mother into letting us spend the night out in our tent in the back yard. We carried all our stuff down, our sleeping bags, a can of insect repellent, some eggs and bacon for breakfast, and a lantern.

"I'll leave the back door open, just in case," Mom said. We knew she'd proably sit up all night to see nothing happened to us.

"In case what?" Joss wanted to know.

"In case it rains or thunders or you decide to come in."

"Oh, we won't get scared," Joss said. "Jean-Pierre will take care of us. There's nothing he's afraid of, is there, Jean-Pierre?"

Joss nodded and smiled at him. "He says, 'Never fear'—he's spent the night out plenty of times. Sometimes it's scary if an owl starts hooting. Or if a raccoon sticks his head inside the tent. Or if a skunk comes around. But Jean-Pierre will take care of us. What's that?"

Joss bent down to listen to what Jean-Pierre had to say. He was able to change his size at will. Sometimes he was bigger than Joss, bigger than me, sometimes he was a tiny baby. It was a very handy trick.

"Jean-Pierre says it might be a good idea to leave the back door open, Mom," Joss said. "He said he might have to come inside to go to the bathroom. You know how he is."

I don't remember exactly when Jean-Pierre disappeared. I think it was when Joss was about eight. One day he was there, the next he was gone. It was as simple as that. When I asked her where he was, she said he'd gone to visit his family and he might never come back.

"You have to understand Jean-Pierre the way I do," she said. "He's a real friend. He's there when you need him, he'll do anything in the world for me, but he doesn't want to hang around. He has other things to do. It's very simple, Kate."

Once in a great while, like then, I remember feeling that Joss was older than I, much older.

As I said, last night Joss had another dream. She shouted, "Jean-Pierre! Jean-Pierre!" over and over. I listened for a few minutes to see if she'd say something interesting, but she didn't.

I shook her finally, gently.

"Hey," I said, "stop hollering."

She sat up, rubbing her eyes.

"You should've let me sleep," she said. "Why do you always wake me up?"

"Because you shout so loud when you're dreaming that I can't sleep," I said.

"It was so real, Kate," she said. "I dreamed Jean-Pierre and I were riding horses alongside a river, and he fell off into the water. I went to rescue him. He had on a bright red shirt, and then I couldn't see him at all. It was so real." She shuddered.

"Do you want some cocoa?" I asked her. Sometimes if you drink something hot when you wake up from a bad dream, it helps. Then I remembered an old superstition a girl in my class had told me about. She said if you put your shoes under the bed with the soles up, it'll stop nightmares. I'd been waiting for some time to try this out to see if it worked.

I got out of bed and put Joss's shoes with the soles up under her bed.

"Now you're all set," I said. I told her about the old superstition.

"Good." Joss settled back under the covers. "It was so real. I hope he's all right. Jean-Pierre, I mean."

"He's fine," I told her. "I know he's fine. Don't worry. Go to sleep."

And she did. Right away. That old superstition must really be true.

It was so strange, both of us talking about an imaginary person as if he were real. Even after all that time Jean-Pierre was real. That was perhaps the strangest part of all.

"*I* figure Grandmother is good for twenty-five dollars," Joss said. Her birthday was only four days away. She was adding up the money she planned on getting.

"That sounds horrible," I said. Actually, Grandmother probably would give her twenty-five dollars. She was a creature of habit. She had given us both that amount as long as I could remember. When we were little, my mother and father used to put the checks in the bank in our savings account.

But for the past few years we'd been allowed to spend part of it. Last year I was going through an altruistic phase and said I was going to give five dollars of my birthday money to an organization which fed children overseas.

"Me too," Joss said. "As a matter of fact, I'm going to give all of mine." She settled on giving five dollars too. It made us feel good, knowing we were doing something for other kids.

"Are you going to spend the whole twenty-five on the horse?" I asked her.

Joss poked the pencil in her ear.

"I'll have to see," she said.

"You better cut that out or you'll puncture your eardrum," I said. I know this kid at school who had a thing about her ears being dirty. She was always attacking them with cotton swabs. Finally she had to go to the doctor and have him remove all the wax she'd been packing down in her ears all that time. That's kind of disgusting, but it's true. This same girl also used to smell her dog's ears to see if they smelled musty. If they did, she said, it meant he was sick.

She was definitely hung up on ears.

I knew another girl who had a fungus inside her ear. Every time she dove off the board at the Y pool, the fungus began to pulsate, due to the large dose of water it had received. Funguses—or is it fungi?—anyway, they thrive on water. Ear plugs didn't do any good. Eventually she had to give up diving entirely. Which was too bad, since she'd been planning to make the U.S. Olympic diving team.

This kind of information gives me goose pimples, it's so revolting. But it has a terrible fascination for me.

"You sound so mercenary when you say things like that," I told Joss.

"I don't know what 'mercenary' means," Joss said, still poking at her ear. "I'm just being realistic."

"Maybe she'll pick this year to give you a good book. A dictionary or something," I said. "Or how about *The Joy of Sex?*"

Joss liked that. She imitated Grandmother going to the bookstore.

"May I help you?" Joss, as clerk, asked. "What age group are you looking for?"

"It's for my granddaughter, she's going to be eleven." Joss could sound like Grandmother when she concentrated. "She's mad about horses. That's all she talks about all day long."

Joss jumped to the other side of the rug. "Then we have just the thing," Joss, the clerk, said. "*Black Beauty*."

Joss jumped back to Grandmother's side.

"Oh, no, she's read that a thousand and twenty times. No." Joss put her finger against the side of her nose the way Grandmother does and looked thoughtful. "I think it's time she learned the facts of life."

"I have just the thing." Joss was the clerk again. "It's called *The Joy of Sex*."

Grandmother looked doubtful. "Do you think it's suitable for a young girl?"

Joss pretended she was the clerk wrapping up *The Joy of Sex*. "It's one of our best sellers. It's number one on our best-seller list," Joss said firmly. "And it's only twenty-five dollars."

"Well, that's nice." Joss paid the clerk imaginary money. "That's just what I usually spend so I guess that's all right."

We rolled on the floor, laughing. Both of us could see Joss opening her birthday present in front of Mom and Dad and the expressions on their faces.

My stomach ached from laughing. There's something about a good laugh that's very salubrious. That's a word I learned last week. It's a very good word, very adult-sounding. I'm trying to figure out a way to work it into a poem. So far, no luck. It isn't easy to rhyme things with.

"What's all the racket?" Sam appeared at the door of our room. "Toot and I could hear you all the way down the street. Your mother said to come up and find out what was going on."

Together, Sam and Tootie look like Laurel and Hardy. Sam is tall for his age and thin. His cowlicks make him look even taller. Tootie is short and still in possession of his baby fat.

Sam told me last week Tootie told him he wished they were brothers.

Sam was embarrassed. "I told the kid he already had three brothers, what'd he want another one for. And he said I was nicer than any of his real brothers. What do you say to a little kid when he says something like that?"

Tootie got in the habit of taking Sam's hand when they crossed the street or maybe when they walked down the block where a ferocious dog lived.

"I told him he was getting too old for that," Sam said. "Imagine if some wise guy saw us holding hands. I don't even like to think about it. I told him he'd have to quit it."

Now when Tootie walks with Sam he clasps his

hands behind his back and paces, his head down. I told him he looked like a world leader at a conference. He was pleased.

"Kate and I were just talking about what my grandmother's giving me for my birthday," Joss said. Her face was red. We looked at each other and started to giggle again.

"It must be awful funny," Tootie said. He looks anxious a lot, as if he hoped to please people but isn't exactly sure how to go about it. I think that comes from the fact that he's the least bright kid in a big smart family and he gets teased a lot. Too much teasing can destroy a person's self-confidence.

Once Joss punched a kid who was giving Tootie a hard time. The kid was bigger than she was, but she knocked him down anyway. She took him by surprise. He never expected a wiry little kid to be so strong. Her strength was as the strength of ten because she was so mad. From then on, Tootie was Joss's shadow. I think he would've given his life for her if he could. No one has ever hero-worshipped me the way Tootie does Joss. I'm not sure I'd be up to it. No one has ever thought I was perfect, which is probably just as well.

"Let's go over to Essig's and see how Prince is," Joss said. As the big day approached, she could feel Prince's hot breath on her neck and hear him whinny in our garage.

On our way out, we went through the kitchen and got a couple of bananas and cookies to eat on the journey. Sam took a huge handful. That ride to West Norwalk took a lot out of us.

"Don't be such a pig," I told Sam. Boys his age are very greedy, I've noticed. More than girls, I mean.

"You know who you remind me of?" I asked Sam as we started out. Joss and Tootie were already down at the rotary, waiting for us.

Sam had to unlock his bike. He has a very valuable ten-speed bike, and he wasn't taking any chances. Sam's father told him he'd pay one half if Sam could cough up the other half. Sam never stopped moving until he earned that money. He mowed lawns, baby-sat, washed windows, you name it. So now, even when he left his bike alone for a second, he locked it.

"A very sinister-looking character was prowling around our house the other day," Sam said. "He looked like a bike thief to me. I'm thinking of taking out insurance."

"What's a bike thief look like anyhow?" I asked. Sometimes Sam didn't listen.

"He is lean and hungry and evil-looking," Sam said. "He loiters a lot. I called up the police and reported a suspicious-looking bike thief loitering around my house. And you know what the guy said? He said, 'Sonny, see if you can catch him in the act, then give me a call and I'll send somebody over.' How do you like that?'' Sam can get very indignant at what he considers injustice.

"You know who you remind me of?" I asked Sam again. The lock was jammed and took a while. I could see Joss waving her arms at us, heard her holler, "Hurry up!"

"No, who?" Sam said absent-mindedly.

"Paul Newman," I said.

"Paul who?" Sam asked.

"Paul Newman," I said slowly and distinctly.

"Is that that new kid in Miss Costello's home room?" Sam wanted to know.

I knew it.

"Sam," I said, "you live in another world. You know that?"

"And when I went outside to see what the guy was up to," Sam continued, as if I hadn't asked him a question, "you know what? He turned out to be a vacuum-cleaner salesman.

" 'Your mother home, kid?' he said to me. 'I got a special on these machines. I sell ten, I get a free trip to Atlantic City. The wife and kids included. Frankly, I'd rather go without the wife and kids, but the boss, he's a family man.' "

Sam put his bicycle lock in his pocket.

"How do you like that?" he asked me again and rode to meet Tootie and Joss.

"Get a move on," he called back to me. I had a hard job catching up to him, I was so mad.

*T*he two best things about Joss are her eyes and her smell. She smells like a puppy that's just had a bath. She also smells of chewing gum that's been chewed awhile. I love Joss's smell.

Everybody has a smell of their own, I've decided. My mother smells of Femme, a French perfume she's addicted to. When the bottle is almost gone, she puts it in her underwear drawer so she gets the benefit of the last drop.

My father smells of his hair tonic, which has saved him from going the route of all the other men in his family, mainly: bald. When his father and two brothers and he get together, they sort of circle him suspiciously. Once in a while they feel his hair gingerly. I think they think it's a wig. But it's all his own. He owes it all to this hair tonic, which he orders by mail.

My mother's cousin Mona has a glandular condition. She's been to lots of doctors, specialists, to see if they can help her. So far, no luck. Mona smells peculiarly unpleasant. She takes about ten baths a day. She uses gallons of deodorants and lotions. Nothing does any good. Her glands work overtime, I guess.

After Mona comes for a visit, which isn't often,

my mother opens the windows and says, "Poor Mona, she's such a nice person, such a sweet girl. It's a shame."

My mother has been trying to find a husband for Mona for a long time. Mona is also not a girl, being twenty-nine. Joss and I are on the lookout for some guy whose sense of smell is all whacked out. If we find one, we figure Mona could move in on him, and as long as he couldn't smell her, she could win him easily. Mona runs a telephone-answering service, which means she doesn't have to mingle with people. Which is good in one way but bad in another. She doesn't get a chance to meet new men. I figure if Joss and I really set our minds to it, we could dig up some man whose nose is out of commission, due to an accident at birth or something. Mona wears pretty clothes and makes terrific lasagna. It's only her glands that are against her.

When I asked Joss what she thought I smelled like, she thought for a minute. Then she wrinkled her nose and said, "Salami." We'd had salami sandwiches for lunch.

"I don't mean that," I said. "What does my own personal smell remind you of? Everybody has a smell. Someday I'm going to write a murder mystery, and the way they trap the murderer is by his smell. His odor is so distinctive that it gives him away."

Joss was polishing her boots, as usual.

"If you keep rubbing those things, they'll disintegrate," I said crossly.

After a while Joss said, "You smell like a field of hay after a rain storm."

"Hey," I said, "that's pretty nice."

"The only trouble is, down at one end of the field is a big bunch of cows," Joss said, smiling.

I threw my hairbrush at her. It hit the wall and the handle broke. She threw one of her boots at me. I caught it and wouldn't give it to her until she took back the part about the cows.

We decided Miss Pemberthy smells like old socks. Tootie smells like peanut butter and erasers. Tootie erases stuff a lot. Sam smells like rubber bands and motor oil. My friend Ellen Spicer smells like baby lotion. Ellen's mother is bananas on the subject of how dry skin ages a person, so she bought Ellen the large economy size of baby lotion to pour on herself. Ellen is so busy trying to combat dry skin she doesn't even have time to talk on the telephone any more. Which is pretty silly at her age. Ellen's mother lies about her age. She's always saying she was practically a baby when Ellen was born, like about eighteen. Which, if true, would make her thirty-one now. My mother says she knows for a fact that Mrs. Spicer graduated from high school four years after *she* did, which would make her thirty-six.

"A *good* thirty-six," my mother said, pulling her eyebrows together in that positive way she has.

I'm not sure what a good thirty-six is against a bad thirty-six, but I'm willing to bet dough Mrs. Spicer isn't thirty-one. People, especially women, have such a thing about their age. I know a girl, who shall be nameless, who's always trying to pretend she's older than she is. She went skiing last winter with a bunch of kids who were all older than she was. So while they're lying about their ages so they can get a junior lift ticket to save a couple of bucks, she's lying, making herself older than she really is, and finds herself paying full price.

How stupid can you get.

"Mrs. Essig smells like talcum powder," Joss said.

"And coffee," I added. "She must drink a gallon of coffee every day. It's a wonder she doesn't have coffee nerves."

"And Mr. Essig smells like—" Joss stopped to think.

"Mr. Essig just plain smells," I said.

Joss frowned. "Mr. Essig smells like a farmer," she said. "He's a man of the soil."

"I got news for you, kid," I said. "There haven't been any farms in West Norwalk practically since the American Revolution."

"He smells of the land," Joss insisted. "When I grow up, I'm going to marry a man who smells just like Mr. Essig. I *like* the way he smells."

When Joss makes up her mind about a person, it stays made. There's no sense arguing with her. Mr. Essig is one of the world's finest because he rents horses, I guess. I think if there was a story in tomorrow's paper saying Mr. Essig had run amok, killing Mrs. Essig, her girl friend Sheila, and several others, Joss would probably say, "Poor man, it wasn't his fault." As long as he didn't knock off the horses while he was running amok, that is.

*W*e spent the entire weekend getting the garage ready for Prince. If anyone had wanted to, they could've eaten off the floor. Joss took a couple of blankets from the storage closet where my mother had put them for the summer and spread them in a corner.

"Just in case we have a cold spell," she said.

"If I were you, I wouldn't use that white one that Dad gave Mom for Christmas," I said. "I happen to know that's her favorite, plus it cost a lot of money and she loves it. Also, I don't really think it's necessary for a horse to have a white blanket. Do you?" I used my most sarcastic tone, which made no dent in Joss whatsoever.

"I just want him to be comfortable," she said. You'd think Prince was a new baby coming home from the hospital, the way she was carrying on.

Joss got the scrub pail from under the kitchen sink and filled it with water in case Prince was parched after his trip.

"After all," she said, "he isn't used to taking such long trips. West Norwalk isn't exactly around the corner."

"Tell me," I said. "I ride my bike there quite frequently. The muscles on my brawny legs are strong as iron bands from pedaling up Comstock Hill."

"Kate," Joss said, "this is going to be the best time in my whole life. When I get Prince, I will be in paradise. That's all there is to it." She hugged herself. Her eyes were gigantic. Joss's face is narrow anyway, and when she is happy, the way she was now, her eyes seem to expand and take up more room than ordinarily.

"Listen," I said, "what if something happens and Grandmother really doesn't send you the money? Or suppose Prince broke a leg or something? It's not good to count so much on something."

"It doesn't matter what you say, Kate. Nothing will stop me having Prince here. Nothing. It is ordained." Joss knelt down and touched her forehead to the garage floor. We had seen a guru do this on television only last week. He was a pretty fat guru, and touching his head to the floor didn't come easy.

"Yeah, well, it's also ordained that you better put that blanket back in the closet before Mom or Dad sees it on the garage floor," I said. "If they do, it is ordained that you'll get a few smacks on your rear end."

Reluctantly Joss decided maybe I was right. At dinner that night she told my father how neat and clean and shining our garage was, in anticipation of the great event.

"And, Dad," she said seriously, "I don't want you to put your car in the garage. Not now, anyway. Not until after Prince goes back to Mr. Essig.''

''Is that so?'' I could tell my father was amused. He has a way of tensing the corners of his mouth when he doesn't want to laugh. ''What do you suggest I do with it? Leave it at the station and take a taxi?''

''Well''—Joss rested her chin in her hands—''that's not a bad idea. I was thinking you could leave it out on the street. Just for a little bit, Dad. Only a week. That's not too much to ask, is it?''

My father was such a pushover. He rubbed the back of his hand back and forth over Joss's cheek.

''I guess not,'' he said. ''But what do I get out of it? What'll you do for me?''

Joss considered for such a long time that my mother finally said, ''Eat before it gets cold.''

''I'll tell you,'' she said slowly, waving her fork in the air, ''you can have the best thing of all, the very best.''

''What's that?'' my father asked.

''You,'' said Joss, as if she were giving him the Nobel peace prize, ''can have the first ride on Prince.''

We all sat around the table and smiled at one another. I don't know why, but at that moment our family was probably the happiest we had ever been.

''I'm overwhelmed,'' my father said.

June

You know how the longer you wait for something, the further off it seems to get? First we had to get school out of the way. Then came Prince. The time dragged until I could hardly stand it. Suddenly school was over. The last day was always fun. Everybody milled around the playground, comparing marks and talking about what they were going to do for the summer. A couple of girls were going to camp. Some of my friends had baby-sitting jobs. The Adams boys were going to visit Disney World.

"My sister is renting a horse," I said when people asked me what my plans were. I didn't tell them it was just for a week. "And I have a lot of writing to do," I added importantly.

It was funny how many kids said, "Are you going to write about the horse?" I hadn't thought about it, to tell the truth. Prince was a nice horse but not what I would term inspiring. No Black Beauty, he. Yesterday I was reading about a famous author who said he wrote five different things at the same time. He keeps a separate folder for each work. He's in the process of writing a short story, a play, a novel, an autobiography, and something else—I forget what. I should think he'd get awfully confused, but he says he doesn't. I would.

Tootie passed his reading test and his spelling and even his arithmetic. He's a new man. He carried his report card around in his back pocket in case anyone wanted to see it. He smiled all the time. When Tootie smiles, his cheeks tuck themselves up under his eyes. It's a most amazing sight. Then he chuckles. It's a treat to hear him. No one chuckles like Tootie. Joss has tried to imitate him. She can't even come close. It's a unique sound.

The day school closed, he came to our house. When Joss saw him coming up the walk, she said to my mother, "Ask to see his report card, Mom. He's so proud."

"My, that's wonderful!" my mother exclaimed. "I never thought you had it in you, Tootie!"

"Neither did I," he said. "My mother and father will probably flop on the floor when they see it."

My mother and Joss went out of the kitchen, and suddenly Tootie's mouth was so close to my ear his breath tickled. "Kate," he whispered, first looking to the right, then to the left, to make sure we were alone, "I want to show you my present for Joss."

"I think the coast is clear," I said. Tootie pulled a rock out of his pocket.

"It's a heart," he said. It did look a lot like a heart except for one side that was sort of sharp and pointed. The other side was perfect.

"That's terrific," I said. "Where'd you get it?"

"I went to visit my aunt and uncle, and we went for a walk on the beach, and there it was. I wasn't even looking. My uncle really found it," Tootie admitted. "He said I could have it. I like it so much I want to keep it for myself."

"Why don't you then?" I said. "You can give her something else."

"No," Tootie said. I could tell he'd thought about this a lot. "It's for Joss. It's the thing I like best in the world of my own, so it's for Joss."

I thought that was pretty nice. "You're a good man, Toot," I told him. We shook hands. I don't know why. I felt like touching him, and I didn't know how else to do it. He was too old to hug.

Have you ever had a day when everything seems to go right? I mean, nothing you could do was wrong? It's the most amazing experience. It gives you a feeling of such goodwill you can hardly stand it. Everybody you meet smiles and says something pleasant. The sun shines, and all the dogs along the way wag their tails, and when you wash your hair it lies flat instead of frizzing up.

I've had plenty of the other kind too. You wake up feeling mean, and your shoelace breaks, and there's no more toothpaste so you have to use salt, and your mother hollers at you for something you didn't even do. Chances are the whole day will be like that.

The first kind is better.

On the morning of her birthday, Joss was up with the sun. She tried to be quiet, but I heard her go. The birds were making an awful lot of noise. Once I heard the screen door slam—it made almost as much noise as the birds—I couldn't get back to sleep. I got up and leaned on the windowsill. From there I could see Joss skipping over the lawn. She curved her arms and tilted her head. I knew she was pretending she was a ballet dancer. I have pretended the same thing on occasion.

She rolled down the hill and lay spread eagle, looking up at the sky. I was glad she didn't know I was watching her. That would've spoiled everything. People act different if they think they're being watched. As it was, Joss was absolutely free of anything except her pleasure and the fact that today was her birthday. She was eleven and something marvelous was about to happen to her.

I was tempted to call out or even to put on my shorts and join her. But I figured she wanted to be alone. If she had to share this moment, it wouldn't be the same. There are times when a person is so glad to be alive and breathing and smelling and feeling that another human being is in the way. I've been like that once or twice. I think that's what being happy means.

I went back to bed and closed my eyes. Sometimes early morning is the best time of day for writing. I have a typewriter which I'm fond of using, but I was afraid the noise might wake up my mother and father. I keep a pad and pencil on the bedside table in case I wake in the middle of the night with some really terriffic idea or line in a poem. I got this idea from my English teacher, who said some of the best, most creative ideas come when you're lying awake in the night, and if you don't jot them down immediately, by morning you will have forgotten. I think this is sound advice. The only trouble is I never wake in the middle of the night. I know a lot of people have trouble sleeping on account of all the ads for sleeping medicine they run on TV. I imagine that's for old people or someone who forgot to go to the bathroom or who is having an attack of acid indigestion. There must be a lot of the latter around too, if you can believe the TV ads.

When I went down to breakfast, my father was sitting at the table by himself.

"What is so rare as a day in June?" He was eating two boiled eggs because it was Saturday. He always has two eggs on Saturday and one the other days of the week. No one can boil an egg the way he does, according to him. Not too slippery, yet not too hard. It's a real knack.

"I don't know, what is?" Joss said. She banged the screen door again, coming in.

"What is what?" he asked.

"So rare as a day in June," she said.

"A rhetorical question, my love," he answered. "I can't decide whether to play golf or mow the lawn. With two big, strong girls sitting around doing nothing but eating bonbons, I don't see why I should have to mow the lawn. Do you?"

"Dad," Joss said, "today's the day."

"What day is that?"

"The day I get Prince," she said.

"I forgot, I clean forgot. Happy birthday, Joss. But who is Prince?"

Joss looked at him, her face carefully blank. She'd play this game for a little bit but not for very long.

"A new boy who moved down the block," she said.

"Is he of royal blood?" my father asked, enjoying himself.

"Here comes Mr. Watcha," I called. I'd been watching for Mr. Watcha, who was our mailman. "Watching for Mr. Watcha" was the name of one of the very first poems I ever wrote. Actually, it wasn't very good. The title was the best thing about it.

Joss beat me to the door.

"Four for you, Joss," Mr. Watcha said. He'd been delivering mail to us for as long as I could remember. He held up the envelopes and pretended he was trying to see what was inside. "They sure look like birthday greetings to me. It's your birthday again, is it, Joss? Seems like you just had one. Happy returns of the day and many more."

Mr. Watcha is going to retire next year. He and his wife are going to live in Florida, where they can fish every day. Mrs. Watcha is even a better fisherman than Mr. Watcha, he tells me.

"You ought to see Imogene haul 'em in," he told us. "Won the tuna contest three times in a row. Why, she puts most men to shame." I met Mrs. Watcha one day at the supermarket. She is a very husky lady. Mr. Watcha introduced us, and she said, "Well, I'm certainly pleased to meet you. Charlie's told me all about you girls." She slapped me on the back, and I almost upset an entire display of canned peaches.

"Watch it, Imogene," Mr. Watcha said as he steadied me. "She doesn't know her own strength, that one," he said proudly.

"Nothing for you today, Kate, maybe tomorrow," Mr. Watcha said, handing me two magazines and a letter for my mother. He said that every time. Mr. Watcha is a very thoughtful man.

"I'm getting my horse today, Mr. Watcha," Joss told him. "As soon as I get my birthday check from my grandmother, I'm going right over to get Prince."

Mr. Watcha opened his eyes wide. "That so?" he said. "It's a fine thing when a girl has a horse

of her own. Why, I remember my sister Gertrude
—Trudie we all called her—and she wanted a
horse in the worst way. Course, we lived on the
fifth floor of a building over in Bridgeport, and
there wasn't too much chance she'd ever realize
her ambition. Not too many horses you'd find
could walk up five flights of stairs, is there?" He
winked and went down the path.

"Do you think he was serious?" Joss asked me.

"Open the cards and let's see what you've got,"
I told her. When it comes to mail, any mail, I just
rip it open in a flash. Joss is the kind of person
who turns the letter this way and that, and even
if it has a return address on it, she checks the post-
mark and all to see what time of day it was mailed
and how long it took to get where it was going. She
drives me bonkers when it comes to opening mail.

"This one is from Aunt Grace," Joss said. "I
recognize her writing." Aunt Grace is my mother's
maiden aunt who lives in Nebraska. She sent Joss
a handkerchief with "JOSS" embroidered on it
in big crooked red letters. Aunt Grace was very
old. With the handkerchief came a bulletin on her
health.

"Went to see DR. yesterday and he gave me a
clean bill of health. The DR. took my blood pres-
sure and he says it's perfect for a woman of my
age. Something to celebrate, eh? The DR. says,
however, to watch my intake of cholesterol. At my

age I can't afford any fooling around. Love to all.''

When we were little kids, we thought DR. was the name of an actual person. We didn't know how to pronounce it.

"I think I'll open Grandmother's last," Joss said. She had a card from our aunt and uncle in Rhode Island. Inside the card was a slip of paper which said: "We have sent a donation to our favorite charity in your name."

"That's kind of neat," I said.

"You wouldn't think so if it was your birthday," Joss said. "At least if they wanted to do that, they should've asked me what *my* favorite charity was."

She had a point.

The third card was from a girl in my class who is sort of sickening. She has a little book in which she writes down all the birthdays of people she knows. She never fails to remember. She must go broke just buying stamps.

"It's from Angela," Joss said. "Who's Angela?"

"You know. That girl in my class with short brown hair and braces," I said. "She sends everybody birthday cards."

"Oh," said Joss. We went back into the house. Joss sat down at the table. "If she didn't send me what I hope she sent me, I'm in the soup," she said.

"Maybe Grandmother sent you a book instead of money," I said. Naturally, Joss and I had a fit of laughing, which of course puzzled my mother and father.

"She could hardly fit a book into an envelope that size," my mother said, which set us off again.

"To the Sweetest Girl I Know," said the card. There was a picture of a little girl on a swing. Slowly Joss opened up the card and a check fell out.

"How much?" I said.

Joss lifted one corner of the check and, with one eye closed, she read it.

"Whew, that's a relief," she said, wiping her brow. "It's what we thought, Kate. All systems are go."

"*Why don't you call him up?*" my mother said. "Wouldn't that be simpler?"

"No," Joss said. "I've got to go over there to make sure nothing goes wrong."

My father had given her five new five-dollar bills after she endorsed her birthday check and gave it to him. He must've been prepared. Usually on weekends he's on his uppers and, if we go anywhere, has to borrow from my mother or, if he's desperate, one of us.

Joss went upstairs and got five limp ones from her hiding place. That money had been subject to a lot of wear and tear. Joss changed her secret place every week in case word got out where she hid it and somebody broke into the house.

Tootie was sitting patiently waiting on our front steps. We almost fell over him.

"Here," he said, handing her the rock wrapped in tissue paper and sealed with about ten yards of Scotch tape that looked as if it'd been used once or twice before. "Happy birthday."

First she opened the card. Tootie had made it. "YOU ARE A GREAT PERSON," it said, and inside was a picture of a four-legged animal that had to be a horse.

"It's beautiful, Toot," Joss said. "It looks just like a valentine."

"I was going to save it for then, but I decided to give it to you now," Tootie said.

"I'm glad you did," Joss said. "Thanks a million."

Tootie beamed.

"We're off to see the wizard," Joss said. She took the money out of her money belt, which she'd ordered by mail from L. L. Bean, made a fan from it, which she waved elaborately in front of her face.

"My, my, it certainly is hot today," she said.

Tootie reacted beautifully. He'd never seen a money fan before. "Boy, is all that yours?" he asked. "Are you getting Prince now? Can I come? Are you going to ride him home?"

"If you're coming, come on," Joss yelled over her shoulder. She was already halfway down the driveway on her bike. We followed more sedately. Tootie's legs were short, and he couldn't go as fast as Joss and I could. When we got to Essig's, Joss was already there, and Mr. Essig was bargaining with a man in a beat-up tan car with two bashed-in fenders.

"Can't give you more'n fifty for it. At that, it'll take me thirty-five, forty hours' work to fix it up good. Take it or leave it," Mr. Essig told the man. I guess he decided to leave it because he peeled out in a hurry. That tan car needed a new muffler too.

"Hey, girls!" Mr. Essig flashed his brown teeth and scratched his stomach.

"I've got the money," Joss told him, her eyes shining. "Can you bring Prince over today, Mr. Essig?"

Discreetly, Mr. Essig extended a huge hand and, just as discreetly, Joss slipped the money inside. His eyes glittered with the joy of feeling folding money so close to his skin. To show his trust, he didn't even count it.

"You got here just in time, babe," he said. "Got a call from a lady over in Darien who's having a party for her kids and wanted a nice gentle reliable horse for the guests to ride on. Asked for Prince special, she did. Had to tell her no, ma'am, he's already taken. Told you I'd hold him for you. Old Bert Essig's good as his word, eh?"

Sometimes I think Mr. Essig's seen too many movies. He seems to be playing a role lots of times.

Old Bert wrinkled his brow and scratched his ear. He does quite a lot of scratching, I've noticed.

"I'm all jammed up today. Saturday's my busy day," he said. I looked around. He didn't seem all that busy to me. I've also noticed that people who talk about how busy they are all the time actually aren't.

"The wife and me is going to Trumbull tomorrow to see her folks. How about Monday?"

Joss turned those eyes of hers on him. "Oh, today, please. I've waited such a long time. It's my birthday."

"Well, now," Mr. Essig boomed, "why didn't you say so? In that case, today it is. Wait'll I run in and tell Ethel we got a birthday girl visiting. Ethel! Get out here!"

Apparently that was Mr. Essig's idea of running in to tell Ethel.

"Hey, little fella, where'd you come from?" Mr. Essig had caught sight of Tootie, who had been hiding behind me and Joss. Tootie is shy with new people.

"This is my friend Tootie Simms," Joss said. She gave him a little push, and he said, "Hi," to Mr. Essig.

Mrs. Essig came out on the porch. She had a new hairdo. Not only that, her hair was a brand-new color. When the sun hit the surface of Mrs. Essig's coiffure, the light was blinding.

"Your hair looks beautiful," Joss said.

Mrs. Essig patted the swirls and curls and smiled.

"My girl friend Sheila did it for me. She works down at the La Mode beauty salon. She's very creative. I like to get my hair fixed before I go up to see my folks. Come on in and have a cup of coffee. Haven't seen you all in ages."

"Ethel!" Mr. Essig bellowed. "We've got a birthday girl here. It's the little one's birthday today, and we promised to get Prince over pronto."

Mrs. Essig's eye lit upon Tootie. "I didn't know you had a little brother," she said. "Isn't he cute!" She made a move toward him. I think she was going to kiss him. That really would've finished Tootie off for the day. Not only was she a stranger but a lady stranger about to put the moves on him. He hid behind me and hung on to my belt.

"He's just a friend," I explained. "He came with us to arrange about vanning Prince over."

I guess she got the message because she said, "All of you come and sit down. I've got a fresh pot on the stove."

Joss was inside and sitting down in a flash.

"Pot of what?" Tootie said in a hoarse voice.

"Coffee," I said, dragging him in with me. "Your kitchen is very homey," I told Mrs. Essig. It was sunny and clean and smelled good.

"You think he's too young?" Mrs. Essig asked, the pot poised in front of Tootie, who remained speechless.

I don't think he'd probably ever had coffee. Certainly not the kind Mrs. Essig brewed.

"He can have a little of mine," I said.

"Which birthday is this?" Mrs. Essig said, putting the carton of milk on the table. She hardly ever sat down, I noticed. Mostly she circled the table, making sure everyone had what they wanted. She was a good hostess.

"I'm eleven," Joss said.

"Eleven," she said. "I remember clear as day when I was eleven. My brother Mike and his girl friend took me to Sherwood Island for the day. We had soda and cooked hot dogs and played soft ball. Afterwards they took me to the movies. Mike bought two bags of popcorn, one for them and one just for me." She smiled, remembering. "Wait a sec," she said and went into her bedroom. We heard her opening drawers. Tootie took a sip of my coffee which had plenty of milk and sugar in it. He made a face. I could tell he wanted to spit the coffee out, but I wouldn't let him. "Swallow it!" I hissed, and he did, although he looked a bit shaky.

"Just a little something for you," Mrs. Essig said. She handed Joss a box wrapped in silver paper.

"You didn't have to do that," Joss said, her face getting pink.

"I wanted to," Mrs. Essig said.

"It's beautiful," Joss said, opening the package. Mrs. Essig had given her a round pin with a horse inside. "I love it." She pinned it on her front. "Thank you," she said and kissed Mrs. Essig on the cheek.

"It's nothing." Mrs. Essig beamed. "I just happened to have it laying around, and I thought you might like it. Some more?" She lifted the coffeepot.

"We've got to go," I said, giving Joss a warning look. I could tell she was settling in for a long visit. She also is the type of person who finds it difficult to get up and say good-bye. I myself think there's nothing more tiresome than people who say they have to go and then stay around for another half hour. "We've got stuff to do at home."

We said good-bye and thank you and went out to see when Mr. Essig would bring Prince over.

"I can't promise right away," he said. "All's I can say is it'll be before nighttime."

"If you'd only given him half the money and told him you'd give him the other half when he got to our house, I bet he would've brought Prince over in a flash," I told Joss as we rode home.

"Race you up the hill," she said. I turned around to check on Tootie. He was huffing and puffing. "Race yourself, you eleven-year-old," I said. "I'll wait for you-know-who." But Joss was already halfway up Comstock Hill, her skinny legs pumping like mad, her hair flying. It was her day.

"*When is he coming?*" Joss asked for the thousandth time. She'd been pacing the entire afternoon. When she wasn't pacing, she was rushing to see what time it was.

"Call him up," I said. "Maybe he's forgotten."

"He wouldn't," Joss said, looking tragic.

She came away from the phone, beaming. "Mrs. Essig says he's on his way. She said he left about fifteen minutes ago. He should be here any time now."

We went out to wait. A bunch of kids were collected down the street, waiting. They knew Prince was being delivered today. The older ones made fun.

"Oh, it's a big deal all right," they said in their special tone of voice, which said they had better things to do than wait around for a rented horse to show up. "Joss is renting a horse. I don't know, I think she said thirty dollars a week. Imagine spending that much money just so's you have a horse in your back yard!"

The little ones did cartwheels and stood on their heads when they weren't darting back and forth, shouting, "I think he's coming!"

I saw Alice Mayberry and Tess Tipler on the fringe of the crowd. They were a year older than

I was and had just graduated from the eighth grade. They bought identical white shoes to wear to the prom. I understand they wanted to wear identical dresses too, but Mrs. Mayberry put her foot down. Tess was stout. She was going to be an opera star. At the drop of a hat, she'd fold her hands across her stomach and belt out "Oh, Star of Evening." Alice sang *Madame Butterfly* and did gymnastic dancing at the same time. They were a couple of stars.

After a lot of false alarms, Mr. Essig's van came into sight. Joss stood at the top of our driveway directing Mr. Essig on exactly how he should back down. We could see Prince's head peering out.

"He knows he's in a strange place," Joss said. "It'll take him a while to get used to it."

"Can I have a ride, Joss? Can I? Please, Joss, let me have a ride. Will he bite? Let me feed him. Nice old Prince, nice horsie."

The voices rose and fell like moths in the twilight. When Prince was installed in our nice neat garage, Mr. Essig drove off.

"I'll be back for him next Saturday," he said before he went. "Don't forget to water him every day. And don't work him too hard. He ain't as young as he used to be."

Prince no sooner took a look around to get his bearings than he lifted his tail and went to the ıroom on our clean floor. Naturally that brought down the house.

I could hear Jim Schneider's guffaw above everybody else's. He had the kind of laugh that always sounded as if he'd heard a dirty joke. The Jim Schneiders of this world give me a royal pain.

Alice and Tess went on whispering behind their hands. They are that kind of girl. I think if their hands were tied behind their backs, they wouldn't be able to talk at all, they'd be so inhibited.

Tootie got quite bold. After all, he was used to horses. He went right up to Prince, proffering a lump of sugar on his outstretched palm.

Tootie's older brother Harry shouted in a gruff voice, "Back off, baby, he might attack." But Tootie stood his ground. He reached up and casually patted Prince's nose. I was delighted. Harry was the main Tootie tormenter in the family. For once, Tootie was the top man. He knew exactly what he was doing.

"He won't bite me," Tootie kept saying in a hearty voice. "You won't bite me, will you, old boy?" I knew he was scared, but he didn't back off. Harry kept saying, "What a gas!" over and over, trying to pretend that he hadn't noticed that for once Tootie had the upper hand.

It got to be suppertime. The crowd started to disperse. Either their stomachs or their mothers and fathers called them. Sam was going to a concert with his brothers. He said he'd check in in the morning. Pretty soon we were alone—Joss, me, Harry and Tootie.

"You better come home with me or you'll catch it from Dad," Harry said.

"Oh, it's all right for him to stay," Joss said loftily. "My mother called up your mother and asked if Tootie could stay for dinner. It's my birthday and I want him there. Your mother said it was all right if we brought him home. You can just run along, Harry."

I could've kissed her. The look on Tootie's face practically lit up the air around him.

"Yeah, just run along, Harry," he said happily. "I get to stay for dinner."

"Big baby," Harry muttered. "Stays for dinner with his girl friend."

My mother called us then, and we ran, leaving Harry and Prince together in the dusk. The mosquitoes were beginning to bite like fury. I hoped a large one would get hold of Harry and hang on until it'd drained him dry.

For dinner we had lasagna, garlic bread, salad, and my father opened a bottle of red wine when we had eaten the cake and ice cream. I had a small glass, and Tootie and Joss had ginger ale in wine glasses.

Joss opened her presents at the table. My mother and father gave her a pair of pale yellow jodhpurs and a riding crop. I gave her a saddle pad so that the saddle she'd borrowed from Anne Tracy, who lives down the street, wouldn't rub Prince. She put Tootie's rock by her plate with the other things.

"A toast," my father said, lifting his glass. "To the birthday girl. May she live to be old and wise and have lots of horses."

"And may she get a good job so she can afford to feed all those horses," my mother said.

"And may she not get to look like a horse the way people get to look like their dogs," I added.

Tootie wanted to toast Joss too. He lifted his glass, which was already empty. "May she be as nice when she gets big," he said. We all cheered and clapped, and my father got up and came around the table to kiss Joss. We took Tootie home, then went right to bed.

"It was the best birthday," Joss said sleepily. She'd been out four times to check on Prince. If it hadn't been for the mosquitoes, she would've slept in the garage. "It was perfect. I'll see you in the morning," and she was asleep.

"One if by land, two if by sea, guess who's looking out the window, it's Miss Pemberthy," I said the next morning. Not a bad poem just on the spur of the moment, I thought. "She's got her nose pressed against the window. I'll bet she'll be on the telephone in five seconds."

Joss had saddled up Prince and ridden him around the back yard before anyone was awake. Then, after breakfast, we rode him bareback with me in the rear and took him up in the front yard. It's a funny thing about a horse. When you're standing next to him he doesn't look that big, but, boy, when you're on his back, it seems a long way to the ground.

I put my arms around her waist and held on. "You're strangling me," Joss protested, so I let up a little. Only a little, though.

We heard the telephone ring inside, and my mother answered. "Oh, yes, of course, how are you, Miss Pemberthy?" she said in a loud voice.

"What'd I tell you?" I said. "She'll blow her cork. She'll imagine the whole neighborhood is turning into one huge stable, covered with horse turds."

"She probably had her binoculars out last night when Mr. Essig came over," Joss said. Long ago we'd decided Miss Pemberthy spent about twenty-two hours a day at the window with her binoculars trained on our house. At her age she didn't need much sleep. There wasn't anything she missed. Once, in the middle of the night, my mother and father had to rush me to the hospital because they thought I was having an appendicitis attack. It turned out to be just a severe stomach-ache, but they'd scarcely gotten back inside the house when the phone rang and it was Miss Pemberthy asking what was wrong.

"Should I?" Joss turned Prince in the direction of the "NO TURNING" sign. "A turd is what I think it is, right?"

"A turd is a piece of excrement," I told her. I learned that from Ellen Spicer. When she wasn't combating dry skin, she spent a lot of time learning what she thought were dirty words out of the dictionary. Turd is a very descriptive word. It's too bad I don't get a chance to use it more often.

"I'll be right back," I said and slipped off Prince. "I want to hear what they're saying."

When I picked up the extension in the kitchen, Miss Pemberthy was saying, "I simply could not believe my eyes. I could not believe these old eyes of mine. A horse across the street! In a neighborhood that is certainly not zoned for horses. Oh, my, what a shock!"

"My dear Miss Pemberthy," my mother said in a special voice she uses for tense occasions, "yesterday was Joss's birthday. She's been saving her money for ages. She's just rented him. For a week. . . . No, she doesn't own the horse."

Between sputters, Miss Pemberthy said, "I cannot permit such desecration of a first-class neighborhood. I will have to report this to the proper authorities."

"I'm sorry you feel this way," my mother said, her voice sliding from soft to sharp. "As I said, it's only for a week. Joss has every intention of keeping him inside our property line. She has promised us, and she's a very trustworthy child."

There was a silence. I could hear Miss Pemberthy breathing. "Far be it from me," she said, "to interfere with a child's pleasure. Far be it from me. I was a child once myself, you know," and she made a wheezing sound that I guess was laughter. "I do hope the animal doesn't befoul your grass. Or infest the neighborhood with flies. Horses attract flies in vast multitudes, you know."

"Oh, dear, I really must run," my mother said. "Something's burning on the stove. Do come for a visit some day soon." And my mother hung up.

"I listened in," I told her. "You did a good job, Mom."

"Well, at least I held my temper," my mother said, proud of herself. We had always been taught to respect old people, but I could tell even my mother and father found Miss Pemberthy tough to take.

Joss came to the back door, leading Prince by his bridle. "Could I have a treat for him, Mom?" she said.

"What's he done to deserve one?" my mother said. "I've got one old apple he can have, and that's it. And listen, that was Miss Pemberthy on the phone complaining about Prince being here. I told her you would only ride him within our property line. Make sure you do."

Still holding Prince, Joss stuck out her skinny little butt, put her thumb on it, and waggled her fingers in the air.

"Tough beans on old Miss Pemberthy," she said.

"Joss!" my mother said, laughing. "Don't be disrespectful."

"Why not? She's disrespectful to me," Joss said. "I'm a person too, you know."

"Miss Pemberthy's mother died when she was thirteen," I told them. "Did you know that?"

They looked at me, surprised.

"No," my mother said.

"She told me, that night I took the package over," I said. "She said her father got married a year later and she felt in the way. She planned on making her father happy, but he got married, and he called his new wife 'Darling.'"

"Well," my mother said slowly, "that must've been very hard on her. Maybe it helps to explain her somewhat, don't you think?"

"No," Joss said stubbornly. "She was thirteen about a thousand years ago, anyway. Just because her mother died doesn't mean she has to be such a witch."

"Oh, give her a break, Joss," I said. "How'd you like it if your mother died and your father got married again right away?"

"Dad wouldn't do that," Joss said. "Would he, Mom?"

"He better not," my mother said lightly. "I'm glad you told me, Kate."

"Do you think something like that scars you for life?" I asked her.

"It might if you didn't have much else to think about," my mother told me. "It's hard to say what makes scars and what doesn't."

Sam came loping around the side of the house.

"Hey," he said, "I'm here to ride the critter. I brung some grub along just in case the Indians attack the fort and lay siege to the settlers." He had on a hat with a floppy brim which was too big.

"You are some sad-looking cowboy," I said. "What's in the sack?"

"Like I said"—Sam was really getting into the wild West routine—"I brung some grub."

He had three deviled-ham sandwiches, four bananas, a package of cookies, and one hard-boiled egg.

"The egg's for Prince," he said.

"Horses don't eat eggs, dummy," Joss said.

"How do you know? Did you ever give him one?" Sam asked.

She held out the egg for Prince. He flared his nostrils and breathed all over it and turned it down. Then he blew down Joss's neck. "That's the way he shows affection," she said. "It tickles."

She popped the egg in her mouth.

"Joss," my mother said, "you might get germs."

We let Sam ride Prince awhile, then we sat under the apple tree and ate Sam's lunch. Joss told him about Miss Pemberthy's calling up to complain.

"You've got to look at it this way," Sam said, waving a banana at us, "she's got nothing else to do but complain. She's paranoid."

"O.K.," I said, "you just learned that. I can tell by the way you tossed it into the conversation that you never heard that word before. What's it mean?"

Sam grinned. "I thought you'd never ask," he said. "It means she thinks the world's out to get her. She has delusions of persecution."

Joss said, "When you start talking like that, I'm leaving. Anyway, I have to walk Prince to dry him off."

"If I didn't hate her so much, I'd feel sorry for her," I said.

"Yeah." Sam ate the last cookie. "People used to say that about Hitler, too."

For the rest of my life, if ever again I'm totally happy, which is doubtful, or completely sure I'm immortal, I'll be afraid that something terrible is about to happen.

Because that's the way it was that last week with Joss.

Every morning was more beautiful than the one before. Joss was up and out riding Prince before I woke up. When she wasn't riding him, she was polishing his coat the same way she polished her boots. Prince gleamed. You could almost see your face in his side, he was so shiny.

We ate our breakfast sitting on the grass, with the mist still in little patches, making wet spots on the seats of our jeans.

Joss gave rides to all the kids who came around, even the little ones, as long as their mothers said it was all right. I held on to the bridle and Joss would hoist them up and sit with her arms around their waists.

"Boy, imagine the mint of money we'd make if we were charging your basic ten cents a ride," I said. "You might even make enough to rent Prince for another week."

Joss's eyes sparkled at the thought. "The only trouble with that is," she said, "I'd feel like such a rotten person, charging for rides."

The only person she refused a ride to was Jim Schneider. He slouched over one day, his hands jammed into his pockets.

"How about a ride on the old nag for a real expert?" he said.

"No," Joss said. "You're too big. Anyway, I only give rides to my friends."

Jim Schneider's face got red and he swore at her. "Looks like he's about to fall over in a heap, anyway," he said. "He's probably got horse rot, through and through."

"I'd say you're about halfway gone with people rot right this minute," I said.

Jim stomped off, using foul language to make himself feel better.

The admiration on Joss's face was very pleasing to me. "You really let him have it, Kate," she said, hugging me. "I didn't think you had it in you."

"Neither did I, to tell the truth," I said.

Ellen Spicer rode her bike over. She had a bag full of cabbage leaves with holes in them for Prince. "My mother had to peel half the cabbage away before she got to the good stuff," she explained. Prince didn't mind. He chomped them up with enjoyment. We lay on the grass and talked about how the summer was shaping up.

"You have a horse at least," Ellen said mournfully. "I've got this creepy little cousin coming to stay with me. She's only nine. I heard my mother telling my father she was a young nine too. My mother says I have to be nice to her. What does she think I'm going to do—throw her down the stairs or something? She probably still plays with dolls. She'll also probably get homesick and my mother will make me give her the best piece of chicken and the biggest piece of cake.''

Ellen put her chin in her hands and felt sorry for herself. Joss went around with a huge shovel, scooping up Prince's turds. She deposited them in a heap back of the garage. My father said he might as well get some good out of that horse, so we were making a nice pile of manure for next year's garden.

"Hey, turd collector!" Ellen called. "There's one over here you missed.''

Joss brought the shovel right up to Ellen's face and threatened to wipe it on her hair. Ellen got panicky and fell on her back, kicking her heels in the air.

"Stay away from me, you witch. Since you got to be eleven, you've turned into a viper.''

Joss made a few more swipes with her shovel, then went to inspect Prince's teeth and brush him a few hundred more times.

"That kid will be a basket case when Prince has to go,'' Ellen said. "What'll she do?''

"Probably live over at Essig's,'' I said. "Maybe

she'll pay them if they let her be stable girl.''

We stayed up way past our usual bedtime every night that week. It was hot for June, and we could hear my mother's and father's voices from the screened porch where they sat in the dark, looking out at the fireflies. Once or twice they'd call, ''About time for bed,'' and we'd say, firmly, ''Not quite.'' They didn't argue. We were all caught up in a net of summer contentment. The sky turned pale green, then lavender, the first stars came out. The night birds sang as if they didn't have a thing on their minds except providing music for us. The mosquitoes attacked, even though we'd sprayed ourselves with ''*Off*.''

Sitting under the apple tree, Joss hugged her knees.

''It's so cozy having him here,'' she said dreamily. ''It's like having a best friend come to stay. Outside of you, Kate, Prince is my best friend.''

I was touched. ''Don't forget Jean-Pierre,'' I said, so she wouldn't know. ''Think of how Jean-Pierre would've liked riding his own horse.''

''Yes,'' she said, ''he missed all the best parts.''

''The best parts of what?'' I asked.

''You know. He didn't get to go to the ocean with us that time. He didn't get to go to the strawberry festival and ride on the Ferris wheel. He also missed the horse show at Major Self's. Lots of things. It seems to me,'' Joss said seriously, ''Jean-Pierre missed a whole lot.''

"Well," I said, curious, "why didn't you bring him back then?"

"I couldn't. He was gone. That's all there was to it. He was just gone. There was nothing I could do. Once I closed my eyes tight," Joss said, "and wished him to come back. But it was no good." She put her hands out, palms upward. "He didn't even say good-bye."

We sat looking at Prince. The night seemed to become very still. The next time my mother called, "Time for bed," we went.

During the night it rained. The thunder and lightning woke me up. I turned on the light. Joss lay on her back, her arms at her sides. She was smiling in her sleep. I could hear Hazel whimpering outside our door. I let her in and even let her sleep on my bed, which was forbidden. Hazel was terrified of storms.

In the morning the rain seemed to have made things hotter. The thermometer on our back porch said 84 when we went down to breakfast. It was Prince's next-to-last day. When Joss wasn't brushing him or feeding or riding him, she was kissing him. Not too many people find horses kissable. Joss did.

"Kiss him, Kate." She offered me a turn. "It's lovely, all soft and warm." I didn't particularly want to kiss Prince, but I did anyway. She was right. It was much nicer than I would've thought.

"Wouldn't it be neat if there were no cars at all, only horses, like the olden times?" Joss asked. "We could ride to school and downtown, and at Christmas we'd have a big sleigh with bells, and we'd tuck in with lots of blankets and go over the fields to Grandmother's house for dinner."

Joss was reading *The Little House on the Prairie* for the third time. It was against her principles to read anything but a horse book, but I talked her into it.

"I wish I'd lived in those times," she said after she read it for the first time. "Life was much nicer then. For instance. Think of Paul Revere riding to warn the Americans that the British were coming. Imagine how that would've been if he'd hopped into his car to sound the alarm." Joss put her hands on her hips. "You've got to admit that would make a very different kind of story, right?"

Paul Revere and the little house on the prairie were about one hundred years apart, but I knew what she meant.

"Let's walk Prince on the road and turn him into Pemberthy's yard," Joss suggested. "Maybe I can get him to look in her window and scare the daylights out of her."

I talked her out of that. We decided instead to pack a lunch to take up in the apple tree. Joss, Jean-Pierre, and I used to build a fort up there way back when we were small and the tree was in bloom. We'd take some old blankets to make soft sitting and hide behind the flowers to spy on people. I'll always remember the way Joss used to select the best and biggest hard-boiled egg, peel it carefully, put salt on it, and say, "Here, Jean-Pierre." In the flick of an eye, she'd eat it herself.

"Jean-Pierre," Joss would say, picking olives out of her sandwich and tossing them down to the birds, "you really must learn to clean your plate. Give him another helping, Kate." I'd give Jean-Pierre another helping of mashed potatoes and gravy. We'd eat daintily, chewing with our lips tightly closed, little mincy ladies at the tea table. Once Joss wore a pair of white gloves up into the apple tree. She drank tea with her gloves on. We thought that was a most elegant thing to do.

"Say 'excuse me,' Jean-Pierre," Joss said after somebody, presumably Jean-Pierre, burped. Jean-Pierre didn't have very good manners.

We went to the refrigerator to see what there was to eat. Not much. It was my mother's day to food-shop. We made some cucumber sandwiches, took a bag of pretzels and two cans of soda. Joss tied Prince to a tree not far from where we were going to picnic.

"So he can't run away," she said. I figured the chances of Prince's running away were about one in five hundred thousand. Joss liked to pretend he was much more wicked and unmanageable than he was.

She tied two huge knots in the rope. Prince was as happy grazing there as he'd been before. As long as he had grass to eat, he was content.

"Now you stay there," she commanded. She threw her arms around his neck.

"You are so beautiful," she crooned, "so beautiful." She kissed him on his nose and we climbed into the branches.

After we'd eaten our lunch, Joss said, "That was a very tasteful repast." She sounded like my father. He's very appreciative of good food.

The scent of apple blossoms was rich and strong. The bees hummed a noisy tune.

"I love it up here," Joss said. "It's so private. Do you remember, Kate, how we used to make Jean-Pierre eat everything? What a little fink I was then."

"Keep your voice down," I warned. "We don't want the enemy to know our hiding place."

Joss leaned down to check on Prince.

"I can't see him," she said. "You don't suppose he got loose, do you?" Before I could answer, she started to climb up and out to a branch that offered a better view.

"Be careful," I said. "That's a long way to the ground."

She kept on going. I heard a loud, sharp crack. I saw the branch split and fall. Joss went with it. She didn't make a sound.

"Joss!" I called down to her. "Are you all right?"

She looked very little lying there. My tongue felt thick in my mouth.

"Answer me or I'll let you have it," I shouted. She didn't move.

"If you're teasing me, I'll let you have it!"

The air was heavy. It pushed against me as I tried to climb down to Joss. My arms and legs were stiff and old. The backs of my hands prickled the way they had once when we almost had an accident on the parkway. A long time later I dropped to the ground. I ran to Joss and put my hand on her shoulder. She lay there.

"I'll call Mom—she'll know what to do," I said. I started to run toward the house. I looked back. She was still there.

"Mom," I shouted, "come quick! Joss fell out of the tree. I think she's hurt!"

"Dear sweet Jesus," my mother said, pulling the iron cord out of the socket. She was ironing a pair of shorts. They were blue. The iron fell on the floor. We ran back to where Joss lay.

"My God, my God!" my mother said over and over. She touched Joss very gently. "Baby," she said. "Baby?"

We knelt by Joss's side. "Stay with her," my mother screamed as she raced toward the house.

When she came back, her hands were shaking.

"I called the ambulance," she said. We sat by Joss. My mother put her hand on Joss's head. Her eyelashes didn't flutter. In the distance we could hear the siren. They got there very fast. A police car came up behind the ambulance. The men slid Joss onto the stretcher as if she weighed only a couple of pounds.

My mother held my hand very tight. "Stay with me," she said. "Please stay with me." I wasn't going anywhere.

They put a blanket over Joss. We rode, all three of us and some men, together to the hospital. My mother kept saying, "There, there, it's going to be all right, Jossie, it's going to be all right," the way she used to when we were little.

"There, there, it's going to be all right."

*N*othing will ever be all right again. *Joss is dead.* They told us she had died instantly. Her neck was broken. There was nothing anyone could have done. Nothing.

I don't know how we got home, my mother and I. One minute we were in the emergency room at the hospital, the next we were standing in our living room. There were people there. I remember seeing Mrs. Spicer and Mrs. Furness, who lived down the street, and Dr. Willis. He went upstairs with my mother. He had his little bag with him. When he came down, he said, "I gave her something to make her sleep for a while. Has her husband been notified?"

I sat on a chair in the dining room. I looked at them. Mrs. Spicer had rollers in her hair. She kissed me. Her eyes were full of tears. A couple of my mother's friends came in. They were crying. I didn't cry.

"I have to wait for my father," I said to someone who said I should come over to their house for a while. "My father is coming right away. He'll expect me to be here when he gets here."

Mrs. Spicer made me a cup of tea. It didn't taste as good as Mrs. Essig's coffee.

The telephone rang and rang. Someone must

have answered it, because it never rang more than once or twice. Everyone talked in very low voices. I waited for my father. I didn't know what I would say to him when he got here.

After a long time a police car pulled up outside our house. My father got out along with two policemen. They must've brought him home from the station.

He stood for a minute, his head down. Then he came inside.

"Kate," he said. "My darling Kate. What are we going to do?"

I had no answer. He kissed me and held me against him.

"I must go to see her," he said. I didn't know who he meant for a minute. He went upstairs, and I could hear their bedroom door open and close. He meant my mother. The doctor had said he gave her something to make her sleep. Let her sleep, Dad, I pleaded in my head. Don't wake her up.

I don't know whether he did or not. He stayed up there for what seemed a long time. People came and went. Once I saw a movie in which all the characters moved in slow motion. Their arms and legs looked as if they were swimming. That's the way the people in my house that day looked to me. Slow motion.

My father finally came downstairs. He looked flattened, as if a big truck had gone over him. He mixed himself a drink and drank it without taking the glass from his lips. There were some men in the living room, men I didn't know. I guess they were friends of my father's.

"I must go to see her," my father said again.

"Let me drive you," two or three voices said. They went outside, and I could hear engines starting up. I knew who he meant. He meant Joss. I felt as if I weren't there. I wasn't anywhere.

I went to the telephone and dialed Sam's number.

His mother answered.

"Oh, Kate," she said in a normal tone, "I'm sorry. Sam's at dinner. Is it anything special?"

My mouth began to tremble so that I couldn't speak. I hung up.

And then the strangest thought came to me. I thought: How can I ever tell Tootie? Poor Tootie. How can I ever tell him?

I *didn't have to. When I went out a little* past six next morning, Tootie was huddled on our back steps. He knew. I knew by looking at him that he knew.

"Kate," he said.

"Tootie," I answered. His eyes looked like the eyes of a dog I'd seen lying in the road after he'd been hit by a car.

"My mother told me," he said.

I put my hand on his shoulder and we walked around for a while without saying anything. Prince was tied to the tree where Joss had left him when we climbed into the apple tree. The space around him was eaten bare of grass. My father would be mad. There were a lot of plops around him too. They left yellow spots on the lawn if they weren't scooped up right away. I must find the shovel Joss used to get rid of them.

"Mr. Essig will be here today to pick up Prince," I said.

"What time's he coming?" Tootie said. We were having a perfectly natural conversation, as if this were an ordinary day.

"I don't know. He didn't say."

Tootie said, "I told her I loved her, at least."

I couldn't speak. We went on walking.

"I made her a get-well card last year when she was sick," Tootie said, matching his steps to mine. "It said 'I Love You' on it. Harry saw it and he made fun of me." Tootie's brown eyes were running over at the edges. No eyes, no matter how big, are big enough to hold that many tears. They ran in rivers down his cheeks.

"Harry said, 'Tootie's got a girl friend and he's only a baby,' that's what Harry said. My mother heard him and she made him stop. Once in a while Harry whispers it to me so my mother can't hear. He says, 'Tootie's got a girl friend and he's only a baby.'"

"I'd like to push Harry's teeth in," I said.

"What good would that do?" Tootie said.

"I better go inside. My mother might need me," I said. "My grandmother's here, and my aunt and uncle came last night. They're staying in a motel. I better go in. First, though, I've got to move Prince."

Tootie helped me untie Prince and put him in the garage. He'd hardly been in the garage the whole time. The whole week. We hadn't used the blankets in the corner. It had never gotten cold enough.

"I'll see you," I said to Tootie. I walked him a little way down the road. "You better get home fast so your mother doesn't find you missing and starts to worry. She won't know where you are," I said.

"Yes, she will," Tootie said.

I turned to go back into the house. I dreaded going inside, and I couldn't stay outside. Across the street I could see Miss Pemberthy sitting at her bedroom window, staring out at me.

I waved at her. In all my life I had never waved at her. Now I did. She disappeared.

Then I went in and sat down and waited for my mother to come and tell me what to do.

All that day people came and went. Some I knew, some were strangers. Every time my grandmother saw me, she'd put her arms around me.

"Dear child, dear child," she'd say and start to cry. Nothing else. It got so I couldn't stand to see her coming. As long as they left me alone, as long as no one talked to me, I was all right.

"The funeral will be tomorrow at ten, and the viewing hours will be tonight from seven to nine," my father said. He was like a conductor announcing the train schedule. "Your mother would like to see you."

The bedroom was dark. All the shades were pulled. I could see my mother lying in her bed, her arm over her eyes.

"Kate," she said. Her voice didn't sound like her voice. It sounded as if it belonged to an old person with a bad cold. "Kate, she'll be our little angel now."

I wanted to ask what Dad meant when he said, "The viewing hours will be tonight from seven to nine," but I couldn't. I stood beside my mother's bed and said, "Can I do anything for you?"

"Just be here," she said. "Don't go away. I want to know where you are, Kate. You're all I have left."

I kissed her and went downstairs and out into the light. Ellen Spicer was waiting for me down by the garage. I don't know how she knew I'd go there, but she did.

"The man's coming for Prince today," I said. "Will you help me get him ready?"

"Sure," Ellen said. We took off Prince's saddle and bridle and the saddle pad.

"I better brush him," I said.

"He looks O.K.," Ellen said.

"It's awful up there," I said. "At the house."

"Do you want to come over to our house for a while?" Ellen said.

"I couldn't. I can't walk out on them. What are viewing hours, El?"

She fidgeted with Prince's mane. "I think it's when people come to pay their respects. They come to the funeral home and say they're sorry and they view the body." She walked to the corner of the garage and picked up the shovel. "Let's go scoop up the turds," she said.

"You mean they put Joss out there for people to look at?" I shouted. "I won't do it. And I won't let anyone else do it, either."

"It's the way people show how much they cared for the person who died and for the person's family," Ellen said. "That's all. When my grandfather died our whole family went. It isn't too bad."

"Your grandfather is not Joss," I said coldly.

"If you don't want to go, tell them. They'll probably let you stay home," Ellen said.

Mr. Essig's van pulled in at the top of the driveway. He got out. "Hey," he called, "wanted to make sure I had the right place. Got Prince ready, have you?"

"Yes," I said, "he's ready."

Sam appeared around the corner of the garage. "I figured you might be here," he said.

Mr. Essig brought the van down to the garage door. He opened up the back of it so Prince could walk in.

"Where's the little one?" he said. "Where's the birthday girl?"

Sam and Ellen and I stood there. I gave Prince a final kiss on his soft nose.

"She's not here," I said.

"Too bad." Mr. Essig closed the van. "Tell her I said hello."

We watched him as he drove off. Prince looked out at me. He looked very sad.

"My mother feels terrible," Sam said into the stillness. "About last night when you called. She didn't know, Kate."

I nodded, unable to speak. They let me alone. They were good friends. There was nothing to do now except wait until seven tonight.

"*You don't have to go if you don't want to, Kate,*" my aunt said. "I think it would please your mother and father if you did, but I also think they'd understand if you didn't."

It had become important that I go. I would never see Joss again. We got to the funeral home about a quarter to seven. A lot of men in black suits walked around. They helped my mother and grandmother and aunts out of the car. They started to help me, but I got away from them.

I had never seen a coffin, but when I saw it I knew it was a coffin. My mother and grandmother and aunts knelt down beside it. They closed their eyes and prayed. My father stood by the door.

"If I can just get through tomorrow, I think I'll be all right," he said to his brother, who had come from Rhode Island.

My mother looked up from her praying.

"Where's Kate?" she said. One of the men came over to me. He didn't touch me, which was a good thing for him. I walked over and knelt down beside my mother. I didn't pray. I closed my eyes and said to Joss, "I'm sorry. I wish it'd been me. It should've been me. It would've been better if it'd been me."

When I got up my nerve to look at her, Joss

seemed to be smiling at me out from under her eyelids. Her arms were at her sides. She looked the way she'd looked a couple of nights ago when I'd turned on the light during the storm. She looked as if she were asleep. She had a little smile on her face. Any minute she might hop out of there and go down to ride Prince. She looked happy and not at all dead. I was glad I'd seen her. If I'd never looked, I would've always been afraid of how it would be.

A big lady I didn't recognize came up to me. It was Mrs. Essig in a dress, which is why I didn't recognize her. Her girl friend Sheila was with her.

"We're sorry for your trouble," she said to my mother and father. They said, "Thank you." Sheila didn't say anything. I shook her hand, and Mrs. Essig hugged me.

Mr. and Mrs. Simms, Tootie's parents, whispered, "Tootie wanted to come, but we just didn't know."

"It's all right," I said. They should've let him come.

Mr. and Mrs. Watcha shook hands with my father.

"You take care of your folks now," Mrs. Watcha said to me.

"Thank you," I said back.

Sam and his whole family came. Sam and his brother stood off to one side, looking uncomfortable and unhappy.

A lot of people came to pay their respects. My face felt as if it were made of glass. If someone tapped it, it would fall into a million pieces. One of the men drove my mother and grandmother and aunts home. My father and I stayed. My mother's cousin Mona was there.

My father's brother said to me, "Come along, Kate, let's go home." It was nine o'clock. My father stayed. He was the last one. When I looked back, he was kneeling by Joss's side, his head bent. I had never seen my father pray before. He was not a religious man.

It's a good thing something takes over and clouds your mind when someone you love dies. It's so awful, so unbelievably awful and terrible and everything bad, that people couldn't manage otherwise, I think. We got through Joss's funeral somehow. I don't remember too much about it. The thing that's clearest in my mind is the sound of the earth being dropped onto the coffin. That I will remember always. My mother and father had said, "No flowers." Still, there were flowers, too many flowers. The odor was sickening. There was a blanket of white roses covering the coffin. I had always liked white roses. Never again.

We rode in a limousine to and from the cemetery. I'd never ridden in one before. Neither had Joss. It was a very classy car.

Afterwards relatives and friends came back to our house. My mother must've taken some tranquilizers because she sort of floated through the whole thing. Her eyes looked peculiar. She wasn't herself. My father was like a general directing his troops. He busied himself with all kinds of little things. People sent telegrams. Every time Western Union called or delivered one to the door, my father recorded it and who had sent it in a notebook.

"People are very kind," he kept saying. "They go to such trouble." His brother Frank stood with his arms folded across his chest. He never let my father out of his sight. Frank was five years older than my father. They were good friends.

Finally everyone left. My mother went to lie down. My grandmother started to clean up the kitchen. Mona came in and said she'd do it. My grandmother went to lie down. I helped Mona put away the dishes. She didn't know where they went.

"Be good to your mother and father, Kate," Mona said. "They're going to need a lot of love and patience." I nodded. How about me?

"If I can help," Mona said slowly, "if it would make any difference to talk, I'd listen, Kate."

I'd always thought of Mona as my mother's cousin and an older lady. She wasn't that old.

"Joss was their favorite," I said. "If I'd died instead of her, maybe they wouldn't feel so bad." It felt better just to say it out loud.

"You know something?" Mona folded the dish towel and hung it up. "I bet Joss would've felt the same way. If it'd been you, she might've said the same thing. And both of you would've been wrong. I think when a child dies, it's the saddest thing that could ever happen. And the next saddest is the way the brothers and sisters feel. They feel guilty, because they fought or were jealous or lots of things. And here they are, alive, and the other one is dead. And there's nothing they can do. It'll take time, Kate. If you'd like, I'd love to have you come in and spend a weekend with me. We could go to the museums and maybe to the theater. How about it?"

"Yes," I said, "that might be nice. Later that might be fun."

"I'm thinking of getting married, Kate," she told me, smiling. "I'd like you to meet him."

"That's good," I said. She wouldn't need Joss and me to find her a husband. She'd managed on her own.

I had to stop thinking about Joss and me. I had to begin thinking of me. Only me.

"I'm going out to ride my bike for a while," I said. "If anyone wants me, I'll be back in a little while."

I rode without any plan, really. But I guess I did have a plan because I was on the way to Essig's before I knew it. I don't know why I went there. To see Prince, I guess. To see Mrs. Essig. I hoped Mr. Essig wouldn't be there. For once, I got my wish.

The yard was deserted. The same beat-up cars were parked in front. I went over to the fence and leaned on it. I'd forgotton to bring Prince a treat. He snuffled and then ignored me.

I went up the steps and knocked on the door. Mrs. Essig was watching one of those game shows on television. There was a lot of screaming and hollering because some lady had just won a car. Those shows are disgusting. I hope I'm never that greedy.

She let me in and turned off the set. Without asking, she poured a cup of coffee for me and one for herself.

"When we read about it in the paper," Mrs. Essig said, stirring, not looking at me, "I said to Bert, 'Bert,' I said, 'that has got to be the saddest thing I've ever heard.' That little girl was like some sort of special person, you know? She was so gay, so, I don't know, so clean, if you know what I mean. So alive."

I nodded. It was a good way to describe Joss. I drank some coffee.

"I never had any kids," Mrs. Essig said. "I had three misses, you know, miscarriages. Like, I got pregnant and then in my third month I lost the baby. Three times. I figured somebody was trying to tell me something. Then the doctor tied my tubes. 'That's it,' Bert said."

She reached out and put her hand over mine. "But I always thought if I did have a kid, I'd want it to be just like Joss."

"Yes," I said.

"When my girl friend Sheila heard, she cried," Mrs. Essig said in wonder. "I never saw a girl cry like she did. I didn't even know Sheila *could* cry, if you want to know."

I started to laugh.

"Did her eyelashes come off?" I said. I laughed harder and harder until I was crying. Mrs. Essig took me in her arms and let me cry. Her bosom was like a gigantic cushion, soft and comforting. When I stopped crying, she gave me a wad of tissues and another cup of coffee.

"I guess I better get going," I said when I'd finished. "I feel better."

She saw me to the door.

"Come any time," she said. "Any time at all."

I promised I would. I might never go back. I'll have to see. On my way home I pedaled as hard as I could. By the time I reached Comstock Hill, I was out of breath. I got off and pushed my bike up.

Maybe Mona was right. Maybe, if I'd died, Joss would be as sad and lonely and feel just as guilty as I did now. Because, here I was, breathing and seeing and everything. And there she was, where she was. Wherever she was. Gone. Gone forever. The forever is the tough part.

I never realized before what a good person Mona is. I like her and I think she likes me. I can talk to her about things.

My bones feel hollow with loneliness.

Suddenly I got the mental picture of the doctor tying Mrs. Essig's tubes. He reached down into her stomach and tied them in a neat bundle, with a bow on top, like a birthday present. I smiled to myself. Joss would've gotten a kick out of that.

July

I had a letter from Mrs. Mahoney, my and Joss's teacher in third grade. She wrote: "I know that right now it seems as if there were no happiness or joy in the world and no chance of any. But, believe me, Kate, in years to come you'll remember Joss and the things you did together and you'll get pleasure from your memories. You'll tell your own children about your sister and about how much you loved her. You might even name one of your daughters Joss. And every time you say the name you'll think of her. I'll remember you in my prayers. Bertha Mahoney."

I threw the letter in the wastebasket. What good would prayers do? Then I took it out and put it with my other correspondence.

I had one letter from Joss. Last year she went to riding camp for two weeks. It was the only time we had ever been apart. Joss's letter said: "Dear Kate, Except for riding, I hate it here. I miss you. The chow stinks. We have a neat counselor. Her name is Barbie. Love, Joss."

When Sam went to the Statue of Liberty, he sent me a postcard. "This is some big broad," he wrote. "A lot of walking to get to the top. And when you do, they won't let you in her arm—only her head. Big deal."

My collection included a couple of letters from my grandparents and a postcard from Ellen Spicer from Fort Ticonderoga. I have read of people who have collections of letters from all sorts of fascinating peple. Somehow mine misses.

At first people sent over casseroles and cakes and salads. Mrs. Spicer sent over a casserole with chicken in it, and I think it was broccoli at the bottom. It was quite good.

My mother moved like a tired old person. Joss's clothes hang in our closet. Her riding boots just stand there. I think I'll put them in a box until I decide what to do with them. My father comes home from the office and pours himself a drink. By the time dinner's ready, he's usually had too many.

I don't know what's to become of us. We can't sit here like this forever. I wake at night and for a minute I forget that Joss is dead. I imagine I can hear her breathing in the next bed. Her breath is like a little pulse in the room. I can almost hear her calling, ''Jean-Pierre, oh, Jean-Pierre!'' It's all in my mind. I know that, but I can't stop myself from turning on the light to make sure.

There is Joss's bed, flat and empty. The sheets are pulled tight and they are very neat. My father was going to move the bed out, maybe give it away, but I said no. I want it there. It'd be worse without it. Always before, if one of us had a friend sleep over, the other one had to go down and pull

out the couch bed in the living room. It was a pain.
I wish I had to do it now. Oh, how I wish I had to
sleep on the pull-out couch, which is lumpy and
uncomfortable and very hard to make.

I weep inside my head. I refuse to weep outside
it. I would give anything if I could help my mother
and father with their pain. But I can't. There is
nothing I can do. My mother takes sleeping pills
and tranquilizers. Before, she scorned people who
did these things. My father takes Scotch or bour-
bon.

I hear them pacing in the night. The light is on
under their door. At least when I hear their voices
droning on for hours, it's better than when I can't
hear anything but dry crying. There's a difference
between wet and dry tears. Wet ones are cried by
babies and little kids who've skinned their knees.
Dry ones are done by people who have so much
misery inside them it's like a desert. No oasis.

About a week after Joss died, Miss Pemberthy
came to call. My mother made her a cup of tea,
which I guess is what would happen even if the
last day of the world was upon us.

"It was God's will," Miss Pemberthy said. Her
lips were so thin they seemed to disappear inside
her mouth. "God in his wisdom took the little one
home."

My mother sat lacing her fingers in and out,
waiting. For something. Just waiting.

"Tough beans on God!" I shouted. I got up and

went toward Miss Pemberthy. I wanted to shove a pillow in her face to make her stop talking. I wanted to smash her face in.

"Who does He think He is, anyway? What right has He got to decide to make Joss die? There are plenty of other people he could've decided to have die. Old people who aren't of any use to anyone. Criminals. Murderers." I stopped.

Miss Pemberthy's skin was gray and dry and cracked-looking. She put her cup down carefully.

"I must go now," she said. She could hardly stand up. "Perhaps I will come back some other time."

"You were kind to come," my mother said. "Thank you."

We watched Miss Pemberthy totter across the street.

"You mustn't, Kate," my mother said. "She didn't mean any harm. It's the kind of thing people say."

"Well, then, they damn well should stop saying it," I said.

"Be gentle, Kate. Don't let losing Joss make you cold and hard," my mother said.

"Why not?" I asked her.

She shook her head.

"I'm going up to lie down," she said.

I don't care if your mother did die when you were thirteen, Miss Pemberthy. That's no excuse. No excuse at all.

August

Summer is almost over. School starts in a couple of weeks. I dread going back. People act strange, as if I were a different person from when school closed in June. I am the same. No, that's not true. I'm not. I can never be the same.

My mother says we have to learn to bear it. I guess she's right. We've got to get on with life without Joss. People say such dumb things when people die. They don't realize how dumb they are. They say, "It was God's will," like Miss Pemberthy. That's enough to turn anyone against God. I myself don't know if I'll ever feel the same about Him. Maybe He had a very good reason for making Joss die, but I doubt it. I read a poem which says, "Death loves a shining mark," and I think Joss was the shining mark.

God could just as easily have made Miss Pemberthy die and let Joss alone. Who would miss her? He could even have made me die instead. But I think making Miss Pemberthy die would have made more sense.

Every morning when I go out Tootie is there, sitting somewhere in the yard, waiting for me. We've had a lot of long conversations. If I've done anything positive, I think maybe I've helped Tootie.

"I dreamed about Joss last night," he says often. "We were riding along a big, long beach. I was sitting behind her. She took Prince into the water, then we came out on the sand and I found the rock." Tootie carried the heart-shaped rock everywhere. I had given it back to him. "You're sure you don't want to keep it?" he had asked anxiously. I told him it was a memento of Joss, to keep it always and think of her.

"Do you think she knows we miss her?" he asked. "Do you think she's having a good time where she is?"

I have to turn away and pretend I'm tying my shoe or something. I don't want him to see how much he upsets me. Then, "Yes," I tell him when I can speak in a normal voice. "I think she knows, and I think things are all right with her."

That seems to make him feel better.

Life goes on, which is another dumb thing people say. If you coat a person with love, as my mother and father did Joss, it should have made her invulnerable. Love should act as a protection. My mother thought if she worried enough, if she covered every base, she could protect us from harm. From automobile accidents, drowning, fire, everything. She had never thought of falling out of a tree because a rotten branch snapped. Maybe one of us might break a leg or an arm skiing. But death. Never.

When school closed in June I told everyone I was going to do some writing over the summer. The only thing I've written is a poem. I haven't shown it to anyone.

This is it:

> When it is night
> I dream that my sister is
> Asleep in the other bed.
>
> I wake up smiling
> Until I see the bed
> is empty, quite flat,
> with no other there.
>
> I cry out but
> softly, softly
> So they won't hear me
> over their tears.

I've read Mrs. Mahoney's letter a thousand times. Now I'm glad I didn't throw it away. It's been a comfort to me. Especially the part where she says I'll tell my own children about Joss and how much I loved her. If I ever have a daughter, I'll name her Joss. Mrs. Mahoney was right when she said that right now it must seem as if there were no joy in the world. Maybe she's right that later on I'll get pleasure from my memories.

It's the right now that hurts.